D1256186

Pig Notes & Dumb Music

Pig Notes & Dumb Music:

PROSE ON POETRY

by

William Heyen

BOA EDITIONS, LTD. ❧ ROCHESTER, NEW YORK ❧ 1998

LC #: 97–72084
ISBN: 1–880238–56–X paper
ISBN: 1–880238–68–3 Special cloth edition, limited

First Edition
97 98 99 00   7 6 5 4 3 2 1

Publications by BOA Editions, Ltd.—
a not-for-profit corporation under section 501 (c) (3)
of the United States Internal Revenue Code—
are supported by grants from
the Literature Program of the New York State Council on the Arts,
and the Literature Program of the National Endowment for the Arts,
the Lannan Foundation, the Sonia Raiziss Giop Charitable Foundation,
as well as the Eric Mathieu King Fund of The Academy of American Poets,
the County of Monroe, NY,
and from many individual supporters.

Cover Art: "Emily Holding On To Her Yellow Room," by DeLoss McGraw,
courtesy of the author.
Author Photo: West Side News
Cover Design: Daphne Poulin-Stofer
Typesetting: Richard Foerster
BOA Logo: Mirko

BOA Editions, Ltd.
Alexandra Northrop, Chair
A. Poulin, Jr., President & Founder (1976–1996)
260 East Avenue
Rochester, NY 14604

Contents

Two: The Other

Three: The Host

One: Whap!

The Bear

I was standing near a corral of barbed wire attached to a barn out in the country along a dirt road. A white bear was wearing a path inside the fence. It was winter, night. Somehow, I was responsible for the bear, but wanted to go to town, but had to stay with him. But I decided to let him out, and if he killed some people, he killed them, and I'd be free of him.

We headed along the snowblown dirt road to an intersection in the distance where winter swirled in the white cone of a streetlight. The bear padded six feet in front of me. Would he turn on me?

How stupid I was to let him out, to think of showing him where there were people. I wondered if I could get him back into the corral. Never mind. To hell with all the people.

But halfway to the intersection I turned back. The bear followed, began to play, suspected nothing of towns or populations. He rolled in the road, charged into snowdrifts, knelt on floppy front paws and jumped away, turned a somersault in the air, his fur outlined in starlight.

For now, there on that snowroad in the wild glitter of trees, in huffs of breathsteam against the blackness, in the icicle gleam of teeth, the white bear ran toward me and away, then toward me, his fur flying and swaying in slow motion as he followed me—so far, so good—back to the corral.

The Redwoods

I'd rolled out of bed half awake and flown busy airports Rochester to Chicago to San Francisco then north to Arcata where a friend picked me up and immediately whisked me to Fern Canyon on the coast.

My head still filled with diesel fume and engine whine, I wasn't ready to see sights, but my friend led me a half-mile along a dirt road beside the Pacific, pointed out beach roses and bear scat. There were still grizzlies in the area, she said. Then she decided to go back for the car. I was alone.

I'd blinked my eyes, it seemed, and been transported from city to city to this aloneness beside the Pacific. I shook my head to clear it. I was still slightly nauseous from the flights and the drive. I looked up into a hillside of great unfamiliar redwoods. I scuffed the dirt to ground myself. I breathed deep for the primal brine.

I smelled the bear before I saw it. I did not turn around, did not move. I closed my eyes but could still see the redwoods. Even as I felt the shock, I wondered if this could be happening. Then, I had no way of knowing.

Scat

A friend of mine is fond of saying that seven card stud poker is a two-pair game. Two high pair are supposed to hold up, as they did for him this time. Raking in a good-sized pot taken with his jacks-up against possible straights and flushes that had busted off, replying to a wisecrack suggesting he probably of course knew he had the hand all the way, he muttered a line of triumph so compact and musical that I remember it now: "Does a bear shit in the buckwheat?"

I'd heard other versions of this line, "woods" or "forest" in place of that last word, but this new location catches my ear past the pleasure of the rhetorical question: a spondee answered by a spondee, forced out of an anapestic rhythm, this echoing answering its own question; the alliteration of the "b's," and the scornfully expelled "t's." Yes, this is a line that knows and expresses whereof it asks.

The Cop

Last night I was a cop standing at the hoary exit of a university. My hips were heavy with belts and guns when I caught the eye of a student who was driving out. He'd come to a stop, and looked lost, guilty. I gave him time to drive off, but he just idled there until I walked over and asked for his destination. Ivy-covered buildings behind him were a fuzzy autumn green and brown. Traffic whizzed by on a perpendicular in front of him.

"May I see your registration?" I asked. It was then that he started to drive away, turning into a lane that would merge with the traffic. But I was still leaning inside his window. I was saying, "You don't want to do this stop and nothing much will happen don't resist arrest I've got your plate number don't be stupid you don't understand it's chaos out there."

He had moss and wild grapevines in his eyes, but listened to me, and stopped his car. Then other faculty cops were there, jangling handcuffs. But I waved them away and gave the kid the good news that he would not have to spend the weekend in jail. He could go home and go hunting—I mentioned eidolons and pterodactyls—if he would return to the university the following week. He said he would. He said he wanted to be a poet. He said he didn't see as how he had any other choice. He said he thought he could use some advice. He mentioned lilies found in the stomach of a mammoth. He said thanks, and drove away.

The Goose

1.

I was looking at a 35-year-old issue of *Poetry*. Apparently, two issues earlier, Harry Roskolenko had attacked Kenneth Koch's poetry as lazy, precious, puerile, infantile. Apparently, in the next issue, Frank O'Hara had defended Koch. Now, Roskolenko, unblinking, replies to O'Hara: "There are many ways of cooking a goose, but you must use fire, said a famous Buddhist chef. . . ."

I'm thinking about this as a salient, a rock to protect my rear. Fire as energy, intensity, sunlight released from fossil fuels or firewood. I could say to a young poet who said that he liked poems that just ambled along, that were feeble, that were filled with holes and haze, "There are many ways of cooking a goose, but you must use fire. You haven't cooked the goose, and can't serve it for dinner. The goose's corpse smells, and your guests will sicken and die."

But the young poet might say, "I don't need a fire to cook a goose. I just need a microwave."

Would he have me there? Was this new science doing me in? Had Lascaux become outdated by way of technological advance? Is John Gardner wrong in *On Moral Fiction* when he argues that we are mistaken if we believe that art, like science, progresses?

No. "There are many ways of cooking a goose, but you must use fire," I might reply, "and electricity is fire, there's a great bonfire flaring inside your microwave, and you are the same ancient hunter who has skewered a goose to a branch and turned it over a fire."

2.

"But on second thought I don't want to cook the goose," the young poet might say. "I want it to live, to squawk and shit on the page, to leave its muddy webbed tracks on the paper and on the mind. I don't want to improve it or eat it. I want to suggest it and appreciate it. Why should I burn a goose? I'm a vegetarian!"

"Well," I might say to him, "there are many ways to prepare [notice I did not say "cook"] vegetable soup, there are even cold soups, but the *tastiest* recipes use fire to heat the soup. So, to begin with, let's forget about the goose vs. vegetable red herring argument. Second, you need to eat."

"*Taste*, you said," the young poet says. "It's all a matter, in the end, of taste, isn't it?"

"And don't forget to pluck the goose first," I say to him. "And don't forget, before that, to scald the goose so that its feathers come out easily. And after you pluck the goose, you should probably blood it and disembowel it before you mike it."

"I'd have to kill it first," he says. "I don't want to kill it. Anyway, it's all a matter of taste, isn't it?"

"How do you like your stuffing?" I ask. "Myself, I like it with diced onions and a simmer of garlic butter."

"Gelid," he says. "Sodden."

"You win," I say.

Sacred Text

Robert Penn Warren mentions in an interview that he went through college as an English major but realized, only when he'd graduated, that he'd never had a course in literature—all those courses purporting to be courses in fiction or poetry or drama had been classes in something else. "I know the dreary hours I have spent listening to one damn fool after another talking about the history of literature who couldn't possibly read a poem to save his life," says Warren.

John Gardner also slants in on this. As you teach certain involved kinds of books, you have to fill in the contact hours every week all semester long, he says. "You can talk about modern history and you can talk about existentialism. You can talk about Freud, post-modernism, Marx, the theory behind atomic fission. . . . You get farther and farther from a sense of what makes a good book." The poetry of poetry becomes lost in the historical-biographical-philosophical gloss-shuffle, that apparently pleasant but basically grim, rootless, aimless, quasi-literary academic dance. The books adopted for classes are those that seem to need all the research cards that transmogrified to doctoral hood.

But this does not happen because college professors need to show off or need to hold the hammer of their learning over their students' heads (though we've all witnessed various perversities and aberrations in Professor X or Professor Z). It happens because 1/ there *is* the matter of needing to talk about *something* in class (even thoughtful silences during which poetry itself may be taking place seem to be feared in most classrooms, as though they were dead television airtime, as though the professor had forgotten his lines or was revealing that his sources and resources were painfully shallow); 2/ it *is*—let us say it and then go on from there—impossible to talk about the miracle itself, the vivid and disturbingly atonal jangling or harmonious dream or some synthesis of these created in the reader-listener by the literature itself. Our critical speech may be fission, but our incendiary contact with literature becomes fusion. Joyce Carol Oates describes the writer's dream to make a "sacred text": "language that constitutes an indissoluble reality of its own—human in origin, more-than-human in essence." Such a text cannot be pried apart with a can-opener. It does what it says transparently. At the same time, we are able to speak of only one of its elements at a time even as we aspire toward an articulation of the fusion, the wholeness we feel when in the presence of works of primal intensity. "More-than-human in essence," Oates says. I think of that seamless moment of impenetrable, pure poetry in Frost's "After Apple Picking," "Essence of winter sleep is on the night," a line fathomless and profound, indissoluble, not quite making English, itself sacred and the essence of itself.

On a Line by Whitman

I've just now checked out in my variorum edition of his printed poems my favorite line in all of Walt Whitman. My suspicion about the line has been confirmed more definitely than I could have hoped. I've suspected that the line came to Walt musically, all at once, firm, absolute, irrefutable, perfect. I still can't prove this—the manuscript from which Walt himself helped set the first edition of *Leaves of Grass* probably spontaneously combusted or was lost or sold to a ragman or ascended to heaven or otherwise disappeared from the Brooklyn printing shop of James and Thomas Rome long ago, and, of course, he could have drafted the line in a lost notebook or on another sheet of paper, or he could have revised the line in his mind until he had it the way we now have it—I can't prove that it came to him all-of-a-piece, but can see for sure that he never adjusted the line in any way for any of the other eight printings of the *Leaves* that appeared during his lifetime. He revised several preceding lines and several succeeding lines, but not this one.

The line I love appears near the end of the poem that came to be called "The Sleepers." The eighth and final section opens, "The sleepers are very beautiful as they lie unclothed. . . ." In the second line the disembodied spirit-speaker tells us that the sleepers "flow hand in hand over the whole earth from east to west as they lie unclothed"—we notice intense movement ("flow") in stasis ("lie") here, all physical laws coming to oneness. The sleepers lie still, or seem to, even as they flow from east to west. The repeated phrase "as they lie unclothed" also moves the poem forward and stops it (as repetition links and stops) at the same time.

The next several lines list some of those who lie unclothed and flow from east to west:

> The Asiatic and African are hand in hand, the European
>   and American are hand in hand,
> Learn'd and unlearn'd are hand in hand, and male
>   and female are hand in hand,

The bare arm of the girl crosses the bare breast of her lover,
        they press close without lust, his lips press her neck,
The father holds his grown or ungrown son in his arms
        with measureless love, and the son holds the father
        in his arms with measureless love. . . .

Then occurs what for me may be the most beautiful line anyone has ever written:

The white hair of the mother shines on the white wrist of the daughter, . . .

White fusing with white, child and mother, that color of all colors, a ghost-light here, or angel-light.

The daughter must have her arms around her mother's neck, or must be holding her mother's head. The movement of color is from mother to daughter, but there is stasis again, a simultaneity and a sharing of the light.

Sixteen syllables. Two phrases, fulcrum verb, two phrases. A comma breaks into each of the several previous lines, but not into this one—it's as though Walt could not separate mother and daughter by as much as a breath-pause.

I hear the three long i's, the four r's, especially, and the four "the's." I wonder how Walt pronounced "the." Probably in my own Long Island way, not rhyming with a long e, but with the first syllable of "mother." If so, there are no long vowels but the i in this line, the "I" with which Walt identifies himself with all sleepers, with which he *is* all the sleepers.

"The Sleepers" occurs in dream, in a dream of the great grave of the earth and heavens wherein the mother's hair will continue to grow, wherein the daughter's white wrist will become whiter, whiter, until bone, until transparent. . . .

Only two disyllabic words, trochaic, rhyming, holding the poem together in a love-fall. . . .

A love-fall. . . . The most heart-rending mother-daughter story I know of in all literature is told in the Auschwitz diary of Sonderkommando Salmen Lewental. We would all wish that this story had taken place only in the realm of sleep.

A mother was sitting with her daughter, they both spoke in Polish. She sat helplessly, spoke so softly that she could hardly be heard. She was clasping the head of her daughter with her hands and hugging her tightly. [She spoke:] "In an hour we both shall die. What tragedy. My dearest, my last hope will die with you." She sat . . . immersed in thought, with wide open, dimmed eyes. . . . After some minutes she came to and continued to speak. "On account of you my pain is so great that I am dying when I think of it." She let down her stiff arms and her daughter's head sank down upon her mother's knees. A shiver passed through the body of the young girl, she called desperately, "Mama!" And she spoke no more, those were her last words. The order was given to conduct them all into the road leading to the crematorium. . . . I quickly vanished from that place, I did not see the further course of events.

In mysterious ways, it is as though Whitman's visionary poem knew of the mothers and daughters of Auschwitz; however, "The Sleepers" is ultimately a psalm of spiritual balm and transcendence. During the line I've focused on, I think first of an infant or child with her mother, but the mother's hair is white, grandmotherly, so I think of an older daughter, in her twenties, or fifties, her mother's hair white, white but active, a white moon shining on a bare wrist. . . .

Within the poem, I connect this line with so much else, but especially with the story of the "red squaw" who comes "to the old homestead." Walt's mother loves her ("The more she looked upon her, the more she loved her,") and after the Indian woman, the lost soul-daughter, leaves, the dreamer's mother "was loth to have her go away, / All the week she thought of her, . . . she watched for her many a month, / She remembered her many a winter and many a summer, / But the red squaw never came nor was heard of there again." *There*. She was never heard of there again. But in sleep all is restored, and "The white hair of the mother shines on the white wrist of the daughter."

Rilke: A Little Stone

Between 1903 and 1908 Rainer Maria Rilke wrote ten letters to Franz Kappus, a student who entered the military profession during the course of his correspondence with the already-famous poet. These are of course the *Letters to a Young Poet*, first published in 1929, most recently translated into English by Stephen Mitchell (1984). If in one sense a poetry workshop is a kind of cult—"an exclusive group of persons sharing an esoteric interest"—the *Letters* has become a cultic classic, an object of devotion and veneration in workshops across the country. It shouldn't be. For the contemporary young poet Rilke's book, although written out of an exemplary sincerity, is often misleading, and even dangerous.

The letters are inspiring in their Whitmanian insistence on the individual soul, on the strength that must come from within, on how a loving patience, a long and contemplative immersion in common "Things" will yield beauty and balance. "Don't be confused by surfaces; in the depths everything becomes law," writes Rilke. ("All truths wait in all things" and "Flaunt of the sunshine I need not your bask—lie over! / You light surfaces only, I force surfaces and depths," says Walt in "Song of Myself.") Rilke is profoundly inspiring for his abiding faith as the future, already transformed in us by our past, meets us where we had to come to be ("many signs indicate that the future enters us in this way in order to be transformed in us, long before it happens"). This sense of the seamlessness of time, what Emerson called "the inexplicable continuity of the web of God, . . . always circular power returning into itself," can ready us for almost anything, can enable us to accept *any* future as a kind of inevitability. But in his essay "Fate," and elsewhere, Emerson will fuse free will with our cosmic and genetic destinies, and Rilke, too, often reaches toward what he calls "infinite sound." He sometimes nets the transcendental unsayable.

The letters are also inspiring in their worldsorrow-to-illumination revision of forces that seem to alienate us but in truth pass *through* us, tempering our development in complex and graceful ways. And perhaps most important is Rilke's intuitive apprehension of what he says is the only concept in poetry to which there can be no exception: "the creator . . . must always remain unconscious, unaware of his best virtues, if he doesn't want to rob them of their candor and innocence." At least, I believe, this is the *effect* poetry often achieves, for the poet need not remain, even if the poem was written in a trance, passively stupid about what he or she has done.

But Rilke fosters in these letters the concept of artist-as-outcast, artist-as-*isolato*. He tells Franz Kappus that "We *are* solitary. We can delude ourselves about this and act as if it were not true. That is all. But how much better is it to recognize that we are alone; yes, even to begin from this realization." Rilke's allegiance here is to his Poe who said that from childhood's hour he had not been as others, had not drunk his passion from a common spring. Maybe it would be much more helpful if a young poet did not take for granted such alienation from other human beings but rather, unless later experience dictated a different reality, assumed that he or she was in this life *with* others. Yes, we can feel the tolling bell of Rilke's solitude—which of us has not often sensed, even during love-making, that when we die we will die alone? ("In the deepest and most important matters, we are unspeakably alone.") But we need not cultivate and praise isolation and suffering as the necessary condition of the poet.

Rilke's is often a masochistic poetic. His own sensibility is of course extremely rarefied, and he is speaking his way toward a condition for himself that will generate his own work (as we all do, as I do here). We can understand and appreciate this. But his moralizing to Kappus, and his penchant like the sorrowful young Werther to find in states of melancholy and unhappiness not only pleasure but also *writing-faith itself*, true to himself as this may be, is likely to hold back or disable the young poet and further repel poetry's audience. Rilke writes, "Don't think that the person who is trying to comfort you now lives untroubled among the simple and quiet words that sometimes give you pleasure. His life has much trouble and sadness [or] he would never have been able to find these words." Something enervating, even debilitating, something to be resisted, something untrue lurks in these words. There is too much romantic swoon here. This is not the witness of Whitman's more robust soul that suffered and was there. On the one hand, Rilke understandably says that he can attempt to comfort Kappus only because he himself has suffered; on the other hand, Rilke's assumption can lead to a view of art itself that may have contributed to the deaths of Sylvia Plath and John Berryman, to name just two. Young poets should not be made to feel that in order to speak to us and for us they need to suffer. What they need to do is to live. Living will have no problem coloring that coat of suffering/joy/pain/fear/anger/spite/ praise their work must come to be.

I sense another major problem in the *Letters*. Any well-meaning and thirsty reader, if he or she is not to hear unintended black humor and self-parody, must almost become an historical amnesiac. Rilke's pre-WWI and -WWII mentality and vocabulary could prove dangerously unrealistic. What Rilke desired from literature was what he found in the books of Jens Peter Jacobsen. Reading Jacobsen, Rilke says, one becomes "better and simpler in one's vision, deeper in one's faith in life, happier and greater in the way one lives." Surely, this dream has turned to ashes for those of us whose braincells seem constructed from the human residue from the pond at Auschwitz into which a so-called "civilized" people, as we ourselves claim to be civilized, flushed the ashes of millions of their victims. It seems to me that the young poet in our time must start somewhere else than in oracular wish-pronouncements about literature. People will gradually come to realize, says Rilke, "that what we call fate does not come into us from the outside, but emerges *from* us." Our post-atrocity dictionary now knows that words like "fate" carry concepts and memories Rilke couldn't imagine as he penned these brooding and graceful but limited letters: Were the million children who died in the gas chambers or who were otherwise exterminated, were the pregnant women injected with cyanide victims of a fate rising from within themselves? If Rilke in another incarnation reads Lawrence Langer's *Versions of Survival: The Holocaust and the Human Spirit*, he will rip his letters up, realizing he will have to drink and transform a different dimension of historical darkness before talking about our having "no reason to harbor any mistrust against our world, for it is not against *us*. If it has terrors, they are *our* terrors; if it has abysses, these abysses belong to us; if there are dangers, we must try to love them." We know what he means to mean, but we see Himmler laughing and rubbing his hands together as he hears this. "Let life happen to you," Rilke writes. "Believe me, life is in the right, always." Read with our atrocity knowledge, much of the *Letters* has become absurd. "Perhaps all the dragons in our lives are princesses who are only waiting to see us act, just once, with beauty and courage," he writes. "Perhaps everything that frightens us is, in its deepest essence, something helpless that wants our love." Princess Eichmann. Princess Earthquake. Princess Extinction. On a plane of absolute Zen detachment and nothingness, on the plane of Emerson's "Brahma," Rilke is right. But, in general, until, *if* they are, young writers are drawn naturally elsewhere into dream cities or grottoes of the heart where the right thing is always the very thing that happens, shouldn't they travel *this* our plane of everyday existence, our nowness drenched with political and emotional realities? Millions starve. Hate festers and holocausts break out like terrible viruses. Our weather has changed and we must even consider that we will *not* live in the generations of our children, that ecosystems are breaking down and all life will come to chemical and/or nuclear end. Reviewing Wolfgang Leppmann's *Rilke: A Life* (1984), Noelle Oxenhandler says that the poet "spent so much of his life warding off direct contact—sealing himself out behind thick castle walls and endlessly writing letters to friends about his life, their lives." Rilke lives by way of that aesthetic distancing, as apparently he must, but the young poet must remain here with us on this side of the moat. We have garbage to recycle, and murderous and suicidal impulses that we need to call up in the language of poetry and try to understand.

Rilke says, "those who come together in the nights and are entwined in rocking delight perform a solemn task and gather sweetness, depth, and strength for the song of some future poet, who will appear in order to say ecstasies that are unsayable." Surely, it is now unimaginable for us that such a poet will ever be born again or will ever again be born.

Stephen Mitchell remarks in his preface that Rilke's "advice to young poets is, as Blake might have written in the margin, pure gold." Is it? Rilke's *is* a wonderful book. So much of the soul's limitlessness pervades it, so much of the God-yearning we were all born with and with which every poet must come to terms. "Do you suppose that someone who really has him could lose him like a little stone?" Rilke asks. No, but the young poet must feel that stone in his throat now, and must try to cough it loose, but will not be able to, but must try at least to learn to speak, if not sing, with it and despite it.

The Out-there

I am not a machine, but human, and other interests and minutia
intrude—the rumor or fact of an Ernest Hemingway-Wallace Stevens
fistfight at Key West, the fact that Robert Bly leaned over and said to
me about the poet we were listening to, the poet I'm now reading, "Bill,
if you were married to a woman like her you'd die of loneliness"—I am
human, but my reading of poetry is primarily by way of what became
known as the New Criticism. "The text, the text, the text," my heart
and head say to me in the sepulchral tones of Douglas MacArthur
addressing the West Point cadets, telling them that in his dying
moments he would be thinking of "the corps . . . the corps . . . the corps."

But my reading stops short of being "Deconstruction." To
"deconstruct" a text, says Colin Campbell, "is pretty much what it
sounds like—to pick the thing carefully apart, exposing what
deconstruction sees as the central fact and tragic little secret of Western
philosophy—namely, the circular tendency of language to refer to itself
. . . not to some hard, extratextual reality." Harold Bloom, avowedly *not*
a deconstructionist—maybe more of a boa-constructor—says "There is
no method except yourself, and this is what [the deconstructionists]
refuse to learn. . . . They all deny that there can be such a thing as an
individual." Yes, reading is not an exact science, deconstruction or
construction.

In his poem "Sacred Objects" Louis Simpson says,

> The light that shines through the *Leaves*
> is clear: 'to form individuals.'

There is an "extratextual reality" in Whitman the man, and it
becomes part of his life's work. I would even call it "hard." The glory and
burden of any poetry worth its utterance has always been to keep the
channels open to universal consciousness, both indwelling and extra-
terrestrial (not to mention extratextual). Walt's method was himself.
He tells us that someone holding the *Leaves* is not holding a book but
a man. Burn that object to its heartwood, strip its flesh to its skeleton

and what would remain would be cosmos filtered through a self, the galaxies in every bit of charred wood or bone. "I stand and look at the stars," Walt says in "Night on the Prairies." "Now I absorb immortality and peace." This is the central Whitmanian motion, the person-poem absorbing the hard and beautiful reality of the out-there, rocks and intimations in space, each answering to each, the word "star" answering to a star, the word "soul" answering to the soul.

Seneca Country

> *The arrow: . . . [the hunter's or warrior's] highest instrumen-*
> *tality for divining the fate or fortune its use so often decided.*
> —Frank Hamilton Cushing (1895)

My neighbor friend, Adam Streb, seven years old, runs over to
show me what he's got this time in the old Walt Whitman Cigars box
I gave him a few months ago. Usually he shows me junk bought at
"Woodpecker's," a joke and novelty shop in Brockport village—plastic
swords and knives from Taiwan, wooden bracelets and puzzles from the
Phillipines, a headset radio from Hong Kong with a secret compartment
in which he keeps his candy cigarettes. I usually tell him, "Adam, you
should stop buying junk and save your money," but I also remember
when my own eyes lit up for the first time with gaudy glass-studded
holsters and six-shooters, a foot-high piano with color-coded keys, a
cereal box ring-compass with a golden needle. It's in a child's genes to
fall in love with lurid trivia, and in an adult's to say, "Adam, you should
stop buying junk and save your money."

But this time Adam has in his box several arrowheads that his
grandmother gave him. She told him that when she was raised on a farm
south of here, her grandfather plowed them up and she'd found them in
the furrows. There were many more, she said, but these were the best.
As Adam tells me all this, something in me wakens. At flea markets and
auctions, I've taken the ubiquitous arrowheads for granted—mute,
fathomless, common. But now, by way of Adam's voice and the sharp,
symmetrical quartz power of these found poems, the light changes. This
is Seneca country, the western gate of the Iroquois Confederacy. Every
tree is a door to the Seneca longhouse. Wolves and bears once prowled
forest where Adam and I sit on my village porch.

> *I dug a hole, maybe a cubic foot altogether,*
> *& then another. I stacked the second*
> *atop the first, then dug a third*
> *& stacked it. Altogether,*

I dug six holes & stacked them,
then walked into this world to look around.

Early autumn on the path I found.
A few leaves fallen, but most edged
red & yellow in air so still
I was surprised to need to breathe,
but could. Without weapons,
defenseless in this wood, afraid

of what might find me, I prayed
to meet the way back home ahead.
At the furthest edge of sight, a bear
licked a pond to ice. Above,
squirrels demonized a chestnut tree
whose burrs were breaking forth

Through a hole in the sky, the first inhabitants of this land seem to see us here. Adam and I sense back and forth to them in essence of distance. I seem to have been a moving target, but now my ribcage fills with arrowheads. . . . But I will never know them, the ones for whom arrows were a form of divination. I am a hungry ghost, and my words are sunflower seeds in a gourd rattle.

with song. I knelt, swore an oath
to courage, & kept on. Nothing did not
voice its essence, not fox,
night, owl, nor the face
of rock. Later, I heard
the storied people of this place

somewhere ahead behind me pass,
& saw the matted grass
where they had slept,
& stepped across their blackened fire,
but could not center them here
on these my terms in this my dream. . . .

Light drizzled slowly through time.
I returned to my shovel
in a Brockport meadow—blackberry bramble,
purple aster, watery goldenrod.
Six sapling oaks to plant—
my passage toward that skyworld & the dead.

Stats

As everyone knows, university creative writing programs in America now number in the hundreds, thousands of MFAs graduate every year, frocked poets exist in the tens of thousands. As everyone knows, it isn't easy to pick up a literary magazine without finding a symposium on these programs and poets, their usefulness and/or worthlessness.

Let us suppose, though, that creative writing can be taught, that our poetry, however gradually, improves (whatever this might mean). If there is no such thing as an "untutored bard," and there probably isn't—even the unkempt singers of the Beat Generation went to college—then how could these programs not help toward the right word, the necessary rhythm, the understanding that poetry *cannot* be willed, the realization that as a species we will find salvation by way of poetry or we will cease to beat or *be* at all? In any case, let us suppose that our poetry is, all in all, by and large, for the most part, when everything is taken into account, give or take this or that, spiralling upward.

In *Men at Work*, George Will, the poet laureate of our national pastime, argues that the craft as now practiced is superior to what it was during its long history before 1945. "Today's players play as hard as the old-timers did, and know much more," he says. Will's book is an intricate elaboration on this theme. Could even Ty Cobb have imagined the aplomb and modernist intelligence of Willie Mays who, as a poet witholds certain effects for strategic employment further down a stanza, sometimes deliberately swung on and missed a certain pitch early in a game so that the suckered chucker might serve it up to him later on in a crucial situation?

But we have not had a .400 hitter since Ted Williams in 1941, and wild prodigious streaks of achievement seem to lessen as the years go by, for myriad reasons, as we all know—night ball, artificial surfaces, greater team parity, etc.— but no doubt in large part because, as Will says, "systems equilibrate as they improve." If the highest batting averages have declined, the average average "has remained remarkably stable over time. But the highest averages have declined because narrowing variation is a general property of systems undergoing refinement."

Will has abstracted from Harvard scientist and baseball aficionado Stephen Jay Gould who says that competition today is "too finely honed toward perfection to permit the extremes of achievement that characterized a more casual age." One more observation from Will: "As baseball has been sharpened—every pitch, swing and hit is charted—its range of tolerance has narrowed, its boundaries have been drawn in and its rough edges smoothed."

As reader, editor of poetry anthologies, and collector, I have thousands more books of contemporary American poetry than anyone else I know. Also, as you may have, I have experienced a mailbox fecundity that constantly impresses and sometimes disheartens me, by way of catalogues and flyers and postcard announcements, with the increasing availability of poetry and of the myriad honors and awards and prizes bestowed, sometimes deservingly, on its practitioners. Surely, too much poetry meshes with too much junk mail, and it's a strain to recycle some of this poetryjunkmailmush into soul food.

So, something seems to have gone wrong somewhere. In baseball, many giants have left the field—as I write, The Mick is recovering from a liver transplant, e.g.—but their craft, for the observant fan, still flourishes, despite recent setbacks after 1994's strike and cancellation of the World Series, as entertainment and parabolic instruction during just about any nine stanzas. There is so much going on between any two pitches that an essay could easily be written about that interval. But in poetry, we can't delight in records during a dull time, and we are awash in a kind of debilitating sameness, the same competence, the same observance of the same conventions, the same frequent over-refinement masquerading as experimentation. Individual voices are far and few between. In the workshop farm system, passion has been manicured to a game of pepper, wildness has been asphalted over. Maybe the poets who now get the press are too secure in their sinecures, maybe they play with rubber-nippled sneaks on carpets while the great modernists sharpened their spikes and slid for blood, maybe contemporary poetry has filtered itself to a vapid predictability too easy to ignore down there where it dwells in the league's cellar in this world of science and show biz where only a whole new breed of workshop-eschewing tobacco-spitting rookies without university degrees or university patrons can save it, and us. But they won't be read, so they can't.

The Past Tense

Ryne Duren was a pitcher with thick glasses, stroboscopic speed, and a well-deserved reputation for wildness. You dug in against him at risk, busher.

"I would not admire hitting against Duren," said Casey Stengel, "because if he ever hit you in the head you might be in the past tense." At its best, of course, Stengelese was poetry, the inspired use of the word "admire" here (the whole psychology of speaker within it, the reverse picture it conjures of a batter grovelling and twisting away from the plate), the brilliant temporal image that transplants a ballplayer so quickly to his cemetery diamond in the sky. Playing blind man's bluff with reporters, it was when Casey didn't quite speak English that he spoke poetry. "Most people my age are dead at the present time. You could look it up."

And we notice that so many Caseyisms have at their heart this sense of paradoxical doom, baseball being the hieroglyph for a life on the verge of unavoidable chaos and death: "When a fielder gets the pitcher into trouble, the pitcher has to try to pitch himself out of a slump he isn't in."

We might render his Duren poem to allow the title to merge with its body—in *Poetic Meter and Poetic Form* Paul Fussell says that this device creates "the illusion . . . that the poem is so magically organic that not even a part traditionally considered separable can distance itself." Maybe we could play around with syllable count a little, too, suggesting Casey's occult connection with the occult numerology of baseball. Yeah, Skipper, as one who has gotten his helmet knocked off a few times,

I Would Not Admire Hitting Against

Ryne Duren
because if he
ever hit you

in the head you
might be in
the past tense

The Village

William, sitting up in bed, had just finished reading the first paragraph of a nineteenth-century romance by Mary Jane Holmes. The story's heroine stands in her rose garden at evening wondering whether to follow her city suitor to Chicago or her country suitor to a farm along the Hudson. Would it be the glitter of Chicago shops and pavements or the glitter of dew on meadow grassblades and in the fur of farm animals? William felt for a moment that he was going to puke.

He turned to the last paragraph. Our heroine is back in her rose garden at evening, breathing shadows. She plucks two roses and kisses each in its turn, sadder now than she'd ever before been, but wiser to the labyrinthine devices of Love.

"Jane, I can't read this thing. It reminds me of the parlor in my grandmother's house in Roseville when Grandpa was laid out."

"You have to," said Jane, who had just finished dressing.

"Why does he assign such crap?"

"Try to understand, William. He wants us to contrast *The Scarlet Letter* as a romance with one of these best-seller popular romances. Maybe the more awful *Sunshine and Shadow* is, the more you'll appreciate Hawthorne. Or something."

"Give me a break."

"Anyway, I'm going."

"Jane, *where?* Why do you have to leave already?"

"I've got until six to get to Barnes & Noble. The three-volume Whitman is on sale for eight dollars. And then I need to find a pair of earrings."

"What Whitman?"

With Whitman in Camden, the Traubel thing. You know."

"Jane, why would you want to *buy* that stuff? Don't you have enough stuff to carry around like a barn on your back, as Thoreau says?"

"I'll see you in seminar tomorrow, William. Be a good boy and get back to *Sunshine and Shadow*. There's a delicious part in the middle when . . ."

Jane closed the door on herself.

William, naked except for the book in his hand, walked to the window seat and sat down heavily. "And hours to go before I sleep," he thought. He looked down at the sidewalk and street traffic, hoping to glimpse Jane, but she was gone, a particle in that Village ebb and flow of taxis and bikes, bums and students and junkies and neon lights already glowing against the early November dark.

He knew what was coming on: another of those what-am-I-doing-here reveries. And then it did come on, and more powerfully than ever before. It was as though his heart were a home in a country village. It was as though Rebecca Sunshine, filled with confusion and longing, had come in from her garden and was now tossing in her sleep in his heart.

R.I.P.

Someone by the name of Story was hiding out in a warehouse behind the docks. His name had sputtered from the radio. He'd done some things he shouldn't have done, some very bad things, tasteless things and worse, and he was armed, heavily armed, the dispatcher said.

Several of us boarded the launch, which coughed in the polluted water, but caught, blue smoke blending with evening haze. I remember hoping I'd make it through anything Story had plotted against us.

We climbed up over the pilings, ran across rotting boards, scattered rats. In a few minutes, the building loomed above us. Over its front door was incised a legend: "Allegory Publishing.". . .

To make a long story short, after a shootout that seemed to last for a couple hundred years or so, Story surrendered, and what we'd been told turned out to be true. He must have pumped iron religiously for years, his arms were that heavy.

The death sentence was carried out last night: lethal injection of an inspired chemical soup the ingredients of which read like interesting fiction. . . .

Occasions

In artist DeLoss McGraw's painting of "Emily Holding On To Her Yellow Room," the poet appears in a ghostly bluish white. We feel her dream self rising from the gable of what may be Squire Dickinson's residence. The tower-shaped building here bears little or no resemblance to the Amherst ediface, is reduced to a phallo-centric reminder of the Vesuvial spinster's emotional situation.

During the moment of the painting, our time of privileged witness, the poet may be out of sight, sleeping beneath that gable. She dreams herself wearing at least one red slipper, and we can just make out a spot of rouge on her cheek, but she is otherwise a form limned from vapor, an apparition, her bulbous head an alien's, her arms longer than human arms, her hands undeveloped. If we stare at her, her torso seems bent two or three ways at once, and it is not clear whether that bulge is her bosom or her back. She has no neck to speak of, no ears, no hair. She may seem mute to us and to herself, helpless, afloat in azure from which pitch black storm clouds seem to reach for her, and a talon or claw of what seems to be lightning. A green mist touches her head, and, out of her sight, intensifies itself like a promise of the spring she sometimes dreaded.

She is holding on, the artist tells us by his title, to her yellow room, which is magnified about thirty times from the structure below, but still smaller than she is, maybe that writing room of hers, microcosmic. (This room, too, projected from below, is all window, we realize, with an additional green casing.) She doesn't seem to have much of a grip on it—its green-framed cross seems to be pulling it down away from her. Its black ceiling (or the painted emptiness when the ceiling is removed) echoes/rhymes with the clouds, and may somehow remind us of her famous remark to Thomas Higginson: "If I feel physically as if the top of my head were taken off, I know *that* is poetry." We don't sense fear or agony in this painting, I think, but amplitude, and awe. Is Emily attempting to shield her room from the inky cosmos beyond consciousness? Is she determined to take it with her? Does she seem to be being lifted away, drawn away, or do we reach her during a moment of stasis when she is balanced among the forces of color, shape, weather? She has only the slightest purchase on the red gable of her house, an edge of gown or maybe a toe beneath the fabric of her long dress.

(It is winter as I write. My father died two months ago. He was 86. When, at 19 in 1929, he arrived in New York City from Bremerhaven, he sat on the dock on his suitcase for a long time waiting for his connection, a man who was to have a job for him, to arrive. He waited so long that eventually he was the only one left on the dock. ((His connection didn't arrive until the next day.)) He had no English, no money. His first job was scraping rust from the hulls of ships. Now, my father floats in my reverie ((which alone may do, says Emily)), holding on to his suitcase. I think it contains all my poems and this book you are holding, and even you in your own place now who would not be reading this if it were not for him. Where did you get this book, anyway? When does a person become a place? Are parentheses like suitcases? Is a suitcase a room?)

Once I found out that BOA Editions could and would use "Emily Holding On To Her Yellow Room" on the cover of *Pig Notes & Dumb Music*, that your fingers would be touching Emily as you read the book, I thought I'd like to include a prose piece about the painting. Thus this. My paragraphs would try to achieve a reverberating depth, of course, ahem, gulp, ahem, but would be written for the occasion of my book and as such might not be very successful: each time I'd tried to write something for a particular occasion—a city's sesqui-centennial, a *festschrift*, two weddings—I'd managed only to get away with it rather than surprise myself with meanings that seemed to insist on coming into being from my rhythms, words, story. Contrivance. Cleverness rather than naturalness. In Emerson's terms, Talent rather than Genius. Art resists occasions; if art is somehow pressed into their existences, it must somehow swallow and digest them.

(Years ago, in William Meredith's office at the Library of Congress when he was Consultant in Poetry there, I saw on a shelf behind glass a poem by Emily Dickinson in her own handwriting. Her spidery script with its enigmatic dashes (or musical notations or diacritical marks) seemed to slant away from me. This is a poet of slantness, slanting her rhymes, slanting all the truth. I don't remember which poem it was that

I saw that day, but remember my feeling of vertigo and velocity in that still room. McGraw's Dickinson slants.)

(Years ago, on another visit to our capital, I toured the Holocaust Museum. I moved along in line, saw things that for years I'd tried to imagine, was attentive and mindful but was in no deeper state of despair or apprehension than often before while reading a Holocaust book or listening to a survivor. But then I passed a rusted milk can and, under glass, part of the Warsaw diary that had been buried in it. I broke down, found myself weeping before I knew what had hit me.)

Here then, still, is Emily, lightning and those black cloudlike shapes—one enclosing a blue diamond—reaching to her breast or backbone. Her pollywoggish expression seems to suggest primal intelligence. And just what is it that this dreamer is holding on to? (I haven't checked a concordance, but haven't yet among the yellows I've spotted while skimming her 1700+ poems been able to find the phrase "yellow room" or "yellow house.") I wondered. I wrote to the artist. He replied, "Yes, Emily's room was painted yellow and faced main street from one end. Where I read this—I don't know. At this moment I am (with my daughter) packing—I have 15 days to move. I sold my house. So all my books are packed. However, I will try to find this information for you. Do you have a fax?

"The painting you have was inspired by the poem that makes a parallel between Emily and a rifle (loaded), something like that. Also—her storm (isn't there lightning in your painting?) with her family. I believe the picture has a storm tint to the atmosphere—right?"

Emily died in the house in which she was born, the first home in Amherst built of brick. On the back of my painting McGraw has written, "Emily Holding On To Her Yellow House." Room *and* house here, and we might remember the poet's very precise directions for the occasion of her own funeral: that her coffin "be carried out the back door, around through the garden, through the opened barn from front to back, and then through the grassy fields to the family plot, always in sight of the house."

(My father, a cabinet-maker used to say, "If it's perfect, it's good enough.")

(One evening years ago, during a poetry reading at the University of Rochester, William Stafford looked up at the audience and said, "I love feeble poems.")

(When asked to what he attributed his longevity, actor and film director John Huston didn't miss a beat when he replied, "Surgery.")

(& I dreamed a tree whose leaves were ampersands. . . .)

What to cut and what to keep? Right now, the artist is on the move, I'm anxious to complete a prose piece that may turn out to be about its cover art, or about writing something for an occasion, or about a prolific artist's intentions, or about his memory of one of those painted gleams of light that passed through him, or about such witness that persists even from behind glass, or about something else that will not quite declare itself (something parenthetical), but Emily within the artifact, now replicated in miniature a thousand or two times (depending on press run), remains within what mystics have described as the "active passivity" of transport. In Dickinson's "My Life had stood — a Loaded Gun," a poem that has been written about extensively, we find not a yellow room but a "yellow Eye" which is associated with the firing of the poet's creative/destructive force. But this is one of Dickinson's most enigmatic, elusive, ambivalent (a word Adrienne Rich uses to describe it) poems, and always will be, and its relationship to the McGraw painting—the painter is willing to indulge me, but what information could he fax me that would matter?—is as sun-flare to moon-shadow, as is any artist's relationship to his (McGraw's) / hers (Dickinson's) sources, or yours, or mine, as we do all we can to hold on to our own occasions and yellow rooms.

Diamond

By way of television, this story: In Los Angeles, a woman had an operation for a uterine tumor. When the surgeon removed the tumor, he found inside it a half-carat diamond. It had never been the woman's own diamond, but she remembered she'd given birth by Caesarian fifty years before, and that must have been when the gem had gotten inside her.

We like the way a mystery was solved, though maybe the other principals are long dead. A nurse went home to her husband that night fifty years before, crying. Or maybe she wasn't married yet, and spent a miserable evening with her fiancée who had saved for a year to buy that stone. Maybe he later died on the *Arizona* at Pearl Harbor in a flash of watery light in which he saw her face. Maybe he never went to war, and the two of them raised seven children in Eureka, one of whom played two seasons of shortstop in Triple-A ball in Buffalo before breaking a kneecap on a double-play attempt, but not before learning the ropes of the concession business that he now runs at several campuses at the State University of New York.

Or maybe during the operation the surgeon or the anesthesiologist had paused to show the other the gem, and then a machine blipped a warning and they got interested in the operation again.

In any case, it's clear now where the gem has spent the past fifty years. A central aspect of the diamond mystery has been solved, though the specific stories around it need to be turned in the light and told. That's where we come in.

Pupil

One day on West 47th Street in Manhattan a young man approached a store's proprietor & said that he wished to sell a diamond ring. The unshaven man removed the ring from a shabby pocket in his shabby coat.

The experienced man of diamonds louped the ring. The diamond was set in solid gold and seemed to be of excellent quality. The seller seemed furtive & in a hurry to sell.

The man of diamonds cut what might be the going price for such an estate piece in half and bought it. Later, however, when he removed the stone from the ring, he saw that it was badly flawed: a black eye winked in it that had been hidden by the setting.

The merchant had bought the ring because he believed the seller to be a fence or a thief. But now he knew that a con man had taken him.

Process

1.

Before proceeding, a cutter picked up a quality diamond to loupe it, but it fell from his fingers, fell into a wheel on his workbench, shattered.

2.

A cutter was cutting a 5-carat stone. Cutting & louping, cutting & louping, careful, careful. Suddenly the diamond in his dop cracked along one of its invisible crystalline planes.

3.

A 6.5 carat emerald-cut worth at least a quarter-million. Pure white. The dealers bargained, agreed. The buyer paid for it, returned to his office, then wondered if he should have the stone's only blemish removed. The blemish was the tiniest of distractions, only what is called in the trade a "vish." It seemed as though it could be removed with breath-vapor & a tissue.

Now the owner, before resale, wanted his gem to be perfect. He put an experienced cutter to work. Suddenly the diamond blew apart, dust & chips, worthless fragments.

4.

This cutter, a genius—thus often unemployed, for he has sometimes failed—could loupe & work at the same time. Today, at his wheel in his garret above other cutting rooms on W. 47th in Manhattan, he has finished an important job, which turned out beautifully, if he says so himself. He leans back on his stool against a wall, closes his eyes, wonders where he has been all this brief long day. Yes, life is good. He will treat himself to a sandwich and a beer. He will be able to wait until the next rough stone is entrusted to him.

Polariscope

In *The Diamond People* (1981) Murray Schumach describes the skill of the sawyer who operates a paper-thin blade whose cutting edge is impregnated with oil & a diamond-dust abrasive. His job, of course, is by cutting to bring out the gem's brilliance. His greatest concern, apart from a "knot" in the stone, is what in the trade is called the diamond's "stress" or "tension"—too great a tension in the diamond & it could disintegrate during the operation.

When the sawyer suspects such a condition, he places the diamond under a special microscope called a Polariscope. "If he sees a sort of rainbow effect in the stone," says Schumach, "he knows the tension is too great for sawing."

So far, our parable holds, our poem or story (or such a page as this) may be fraught with knots & rainbows by which, by way of our intuitional Polariscope, we know we've gone too far, have applied too much pressure.

Blue Diamonds

On West 47th in Manhattan, dealers use a special double-sheeted paper to wrap diamonds: the inner sheet is thin and pale blue; the outer, white and strong with a waxy sheen. . . .

Murray Schumach, the famous poet, told me this story of his *satori*. . . .

Murray said he had always been a dreamy youth, a poor student, memorizing the enigmatic Mets' box scores from the *Daily News* when he should have been studying his math and Maimonides. His grandfather and father worried that he would not be fit to follow in their footsteps, but Murray took it for granted that he would make his way by default to his forbears' place of business on West 47th and to membership in the Diamond Dealers Club.

Which is just where he was this particular afternoon, drifting away at one of the long tables in the clubroom where much of the world's diamond business is conducted. The inner sheets of blue paper seemed to remind him of facets of water and of a sheer silk dress that had appeared to him during the previous night. With the ear behind his eyes he was listening to papers being folded and unfolded in front of him, and with the eye in his brain he was listening to trades taking place—the sharp bickering, the skills of pace and volume—when his illumination began.

In this room of businesslike bedlam a foreign trader had apparently preempted a seat at the table adjacent to Murray's, one of several tables onto which northern windowlight falls. A score of diamonds glittered on a tray between him and the seller. Voices rose, tempers flamed, Murray lifted his mind from blue shadows to hear part of the exchange: "They'll stand you sixty-five," the seller shouted. "Never, what are you trying to do to me, insult me?" shouted the foreigner. Then he shouted, "Hitler didn't kill enough Jews."

For once, the traders became silent. In this room were many whose families had been killed by the Nazis. In this room were wrists bearing blue numbers.

The man who shouted this obscenity was himself a Jew. No one laid a hand on him. Soon he was sitting alone at the table.

Murray said that he found himself with others walking across the linoleum floor of the clubroom in a wincing light, past the floor-to-ceiling pillars, through the first set of opaque doors, through the second set of transparent doors, but between those two sets of doors, crowded with others, during an instant of motion-in-stillness, he understood everything he would ever again have to know about Casey Stengel, about himself, about the Holocaust, and about America.

Appraisal

You order a diamond as an investment from a firm whose offer & guarantee seem too good to be true.

It comes to you in a heat-sealed plastic envelope, reminding you of a book in shrinkwrap. You free the diamond & place it on your tongue.

Whenever later, you remove the diamond from your safe deposit box & take it to an appraiser who will be able to weigh it & judge its color, cut, clarity. When he sees this diamond, he frowns.

He apprises you that he has appraised such diamonds before, & that because you've opened the sealed package, the corporation that sold you the diamond will not take it back when you find out you've been taken.

O, *caveat emptor*, only a fool's diamonds are forever.

A Dream of Hell

I was at a poets' convention in New York City. I was in the seventy-seventh row in a hot, darkened auditorium, every poet in the *Directory of American Poets* around me.

Just as I was drifting away into sleep, the speaker on stage mentioned my name. I was pleased he mentioned me, that all these other contemptuaries had heard my name and would have to face the fact of my life's work, but when the speaker quoted from my poetry, I couldn't place the lines. The son-of-a-bitch was mixing me up with someone else, or was hacking up my words into unrecognizable constructions. Squealings and disjunctionings from behind the podium, gauche phrases like "once upon a time" and "the green grass" and "a lonely sneaker." Was he doing this on purpose? I wanted out of there fast, stood up, got out.

Once outside in the cool street, I walked away as fast as I could, a wall of bricks to my left, that city, that conspiracy. . . .

Before I woke, I reached inside my back pocket for my wallet. You guessed it.

Willingly

Our class kept wondering what in damnation was happening in Jonathan Edwards' sermon "Sinners in the Hands of an Angry God." We beheld him pulpited at Enfield, manuscript volume in his left hand, elbow resting on the anvil of his Bible, relentless fingers of his right hand turning pages, his person otherwise motionless.

We savored him in aria: "The creature is made subject to the bondage of your corruption not willingly; the sun does not willingly shine upon you to give you light, to serve sin and Satan; the earth does not willingly yield her in-crease to satisfy your lusts; nor is it willingly a stage for your wickedness to be acted upon; the air does not willingly serve you for breath. . . ."

Verily, Edwards' arrows were flying at noon and drunk with our blood. We were . . . delighted. We felt better than in eons, so we smiled, and were grateful, and willingly tasted this honey in our minds. Outside, our century smoked and warmed and rained acidic particulates, but we were happy here in the haunts of this Puritan divine who crushed out our blood, sprinkled it, made it fly until it stained the pure raiment of God.

Outside, extinction. Here, in his inner presence, we could not escape, not even into nothingness, non-entity. Outside, mutant frogs croaked in chemical tidepools. Here, immortal loathesome spiders over the firepit of his song, we didn't get it, but laughed. Tears filled our eyes. We were saved. No pastor had ever cared so much for us before.

Audience

On a Phil Donahue talk show on homosexuality broadcast from London, opinions flew fast and furiously from ministers and hippies, members of Parliament and Mothers Against Lesbianism, from a famous Shakespearean actor and a Hyde Park Jesus Christ. Near the end, Phil asked a grandmotherly type to stand. He said he'd been wondering for a whole hour how she felt about it.

In spectacles, demure, gray-haired, the woman said, "I think you're born with it." A pause, as the liberals in the audience applauded. Then she said, "Like being born a cripple."

Groans and boos from the same people who had just applauded her.

Phil asked her, "But what's so wrong with being gay?"

"Nothing," she said.

"But you compared homosexuality to being crippled."

"I just meant," she said, "that you're born with it, you can't help it. I've nothing against it."

Sunflower

Late one rainy August I noticed that one of my sunflowers, the tallest and stoutest, had not yet ramified to head. Its companions were past full glory, were already losing corolla curls, spitting seeds, drooping over like old women with calcium deficiencies. But this one was still growing its broad, hastate leaves, heedless of its spindlier pals, content (I mused) to take its own time, faithful it would have sun enough before first frost to flower.

Eventually, twelve feet high, it decided to grow its head and became the one sunflower I now remember. It knew when to leaf out, when to declare its thoughtfulness, and in what terms. Those sepals that folded back like ears, those rhythmic whorls of seeds in that giant's face, its infinitesimal yellow dust of pollens—of all that garden, this plant's patience, its unhurried genetic intuitional code enabled it to become something that pointed up my own shortcomings for me. And, falling, shrivelled, even headless, it nevertheless like Rilke's "Archaic Torso of Apollo" kept seeing me, and now keeps seeing me, reminding me . . .

We cannot experience that storied head
in which Apollo's eyeballs ripened like apples. Yet
his torso glows, candelabra by
whose beams his gaze, through screwed back low,

still persists, still shines. Or else his breast's
curve would never blind you, nor his loins'
slight arcs smile toward center-god, where
sperm seems candled from under.

Or else this stone would squat short, mute, dis-
figured under the shoulders' translucent fall,
nor flimmer the black light of a beast's pelt, nor

break free of its own ideas
like a star. For here there is nothing nowhere
does not see you, charge you: You must change your life.

Scareraven

"Among twenty snowy mountains," says Wallace Stevens in "Thirteen Ways of Looking at a Blackbird," "The only moving thing / Was the eye of the blackbird." Such white stillness of landscape, such blackbird watchfulness.

Walking one windy autumn afternoon along the edge of a field in Knotting, Bedfordshire, I came upon a killing tree, a tree of dead ravens hung there by the farmer, his creation of scareraven. I stood still under all those skeletons and half-eaten carcasses, under all those dead eyes. The only moving thing was the sky—and the branches of the tree, and its remaining leaves, and the blowing grasses of the field, and the remaining feathers of the ravens, and my own eyes, and the whole turning planet. But the ravens' eyes were dead.

I reached up to open a lid. I, at first, saw nothing in that tranquil walleye, but then saw deeper, saw myself, then saw twenty snowy mountains and moving clouds, then saw a watery edge of the Lake Country where a boy was clinging to a cliff. Many years later the poet would remember:

> Oh! when I have hung
> Above the raven's nest, by knots of grass
> And half-inch fissures in the slippery rock
> But ill sustained, and almost (so it seemed)
> Suspended by the blast that blew amain,
> Shouldering the naked crag, oh, at that time
> While on the perilous ridge I hung alone,
> With what strange utterance did the loud dry wind
> Blow through my ear! the sky seemed not a sky
> Of earth—and with what motion moved the clouds!

Later in *The Prelude*, in one of the best-known lines of the nineteenth century he would say, "There are in our existence spots of time," and we notice, reading him, the visionary strangeness of these "spots of time." We live lives, in the main, of prose habit and convention, the world being too much with us, but poetry strikes us dumb—or, years later, articulate—when we least expect it.

When I came upon that farmer's killing tree, I saw myself as though from this distance, now, as I tell of it. I suppose I thought it, at first, the poet's thing to do, to lift that raven's lid and look into its eye to see the world. But out of eld stillness, then, I fell past self-consciousness into that timelessness where that other boy I was still clings to the ravens' cliff.

Meaning

I first heard this story about forty years ago. It still occurs to me from time to time.

Prisoners in Russia, or maybe it was Africa, had to work a diamond mine, or maybe it was an emerald mine. No matter. They worked in their rags in that cold or heat until exhausted. And each night, leaving the mine, they were subjected to a thorough search.

Every night, one miner—we'll call him X—pushing a wheelbarrow filled with straw, approached the guard. The guard stopped him, frisked him, patted him down, checked under the wheelbarrow, sifted through the straw for any indication of ore or gemstones or other valuables. Nothing. The guard was sure that one of these nights he'd have X by the nuts, but every night X pushed his straw to the checkpoint, and every night the conscientious guard, arm of the party in power, searched him and came up empty. This went on for months. One night the guard even burned the straw and sifted through the ashes. Nothing.

The scene shifts, liberation, that war is over. . . .

It so happens that years later X is having a beer, maybe in a pub in London or in a cellar in Berlin. We knew this would happen: the same guard from out of his past is there, and they recognize one another. At first they are suspicious and careful—all those memories, resentments, griefs—but then find out that they are just two men trying to get on in the world. A few beers later, the guard lets down his guard and asks X once and for all, "Tell me now, please, I know you were getting away with something, I know you were finding some way to outwit us, night after night with your wheelbarrow filled with straw, though I could never catch you, you can tell me now, what it is you were stealing?"

"Wheelbarrows," X replied.

Happening

During the second week of the summer poetry workshop by which time I had come to expect anything from the enlightened Gloria—who sometimes wore earrings filled with tiny gyroscopes and sometimes wore stockings with letters slanting up her thighs and always wore little peaked caps the color of her knickers or kilts or feathery breastplates—she suddenly stood up in our circle with two rubber beanbags, one red and one green, and smacked them together—*whap*, she smacked them together, *whap, whap,* and threw them onto the floor. "See," she said, "that's all we're after, that's the whole thing!" I threw a poetry anthology into the circle, and someone else threw an umbrella, and then others threw in the whole shebang.

But it was only that evening in the cafeteria in a buzz of conversation that I heard that Gloria's red object had been a heart and her green object a brain. For an instant, all the cafeteria noises went silent . . . *Whap!*

Two: The Other

The Goldfish Question

At a carnival, each of two brothers wins a goldfish in a bowl. They walk home together, their fish sloshing and shining.

"Mine is biggest."

"No, mine."

"Mine is goldest."

"No, mine."

They grapple. There is a balance, an equilibrium of pushing and shoving, but their bowls splinter against one another. The glittering fish sputter in the road.

One of the boys kicks the fish into the gutter, and runs home. The other gouges a hole for them under a bush and buries them.

The one brother may or may not remember the fish, may or may not ever tell this story. The other will dream of and will write of a ferris wheel with two gold lamps in its girders against the night sky.

Which brother are you?

Gold

Emerson says that the poet is "a perceiver and dear lover of the harmonies that are in the soul and in matter, and especially of the correspondences between these and those." I think of the true story of the Brazillian open-pit miner who had a dream of his beloved dead daughter. She was covered with excrement. When he woke he realized that in his dream the girl's body looked like gold in its raw form.

He dressed in white, hat to shoes, and walked to the pit. His friends laughed at him, asked him if he had dressed for his own funeral. But in his white suit this man believing knelt, plunged his arms into the mud to his elbows, and pulled out a seventy-eight pound nugget of gold—the exact weight of his daughter at the time of her death— the largest that has ever been found.

Laws

Do you during forward motion do what I do?—sometimes I'll fill in not with words but with rhythm notations (maybe, say, ‿ ' ' ‿ ', or ‿ ‿ ' ‿ ‿ ' ‿, or whatever energy of continuance [or, at poem's end, completion] I feel), & then go on with the words of the next line that may already have welled up in me. Sometimes, later, when words need to replace the metrical marks, as I enter a writing trance again I trust and stay with my notations, which for a time become a wordless mantra. Sometimes— especially when there's a revision earlier in the poem that changes the whole building rhythm—I don't. Sometimes the poem itself begins for me solely with the rhythm of its first line. I don't know what the origins of such beginnings may be: maybe an aching knee, or a dream of scything wildflowers along a childhood road, or some miscible fusion of testosterone & electricity in me.

In any case, if I never wrote this way—sometimes my notations are not written down, but are in my head—if I stopped & insisted on words, this would indicate that I was pressing too hard for meaning, insisting too much on idea, & I might be stopped altogether & lose what is singing toward me. In fact, I've a hunch that it's *always* rhythm's under-song that must take precedent—even *as* the words come, whether we're writing or reading—or we will never realize that brainbeat *is* heartbeat & heartbeat *is* brainbeat, will never experience how brainbeat and heartbeat together take us to that home place we feel to be the poem.

Our arrival there has nothing to do with certain dissociated *local* laws, like unto such: there's an ordinance in a railroad town near where I live that says that if two trains come to a crossing, they both must stop, and neither may proceed until the other has first passed through; nor, in this same town, are you allowed to shoot bears from the roof of your house during a flood.

Dumb Music

I read recently in the local paper that the high school football coach can fall asleep in the team bus on the way to a game. He just puts his head back, he says, and he's "out like a light." As a semi-insomniac, I envy that guy, maybe. By the time it's time for his main activity, the football game, he's ready. Why should his bus ride be filled with useless anxiety?

Most days I've got a name or word or phrase in my mind, melodious syllables that I can't stop saying to myself—*Diego Maradona*, or *Springsteen and the E Street Band*, or *Blackberry Winter*, or *misericordia*, or *His Thoughts Made Pockets & the Plane Buckt*, or *The Brain, within its Groove / Runs Evenly—and true—*. I don't think of their sense, but just keep saying the word or words until, I suspect, their sound and rhythm lodge themselves in me. But these two or twenty syllables that I keep repeating to myself during the day—even with my inner mind while I'm talking or listening—do have referents, associations with the outer world. Maradona, the once powerful Argentine striker, has said there is more to life than soccer—alas, he's been fucked up with drugs—and I imagine him listening to Bruce or even reading Warren, Berryman, and Dickinson.

At night, however, a different language takes over my mind. Tired, hoping to sleep, I often can't turn off whatever in me is generating those sentences—usually, I believe, they are sentences—that advance, speak themselves, and are gone, others following in infinite numbers. There seem to be few logical transitions. When I force myself to snap to from this enervating and uncomfortable semi-trance and focus on what I've been saying to myself, it all seems to be nonsense. The words are English, but it's as though something in me is speaking in tongues and forcing me to pay at least enough attention so that sleep will not come. Even while I'm counting sheep or relaxing muscles from toes to forehead, the sentences begin again, rhythm after rhythm, a stupid lack of control in me, I've thought. I've thought that I should be able to empty my mind, should be able to have these flying fish brain themselves against the black deck of sleep. But the sentences keep flying, hour after hour, variable but somehow measured, a semi-circling of headless pigeons, a confused current of nondescript flotsam and jetsam. I'm convinced that these sentences are not poetry. If I had a transcript of a night's production, I'm sure I would consider all hundred or three hundred pages to be just interesting gibberish with only the occasional chance coherence of speeded-up automatic writing.

In *Vision and Resonance: Two Senses of Poetic Form*, John Hollander quotes from George Darley's introduction to an 1840 edition of Beaumont and Fletcher:

> Every true poet has a *song in his mind*, the notes of which, little as they precede his thoughts—so little as to seem simultaneous with them—do precede, suggest, and inspire many of these, modify and beautify them. That poet who has none of this dumb music going on within him, will neither produce any by his versification, not prove an imaginative or impassioned writer: he will want the harmonizer which atunes heart, and mind, and soul, the mainspring that sets them in movement together. Rhythm, thus, as an enrapturer of the poet, mediately exalts him as a creator, and augments all his powers. . . . It is the poet's latent inspirer. . . .

I can run or bicycle for hours during the day, or help a neighbor wheelbarrow twenty tons of rock to his back line, but still find myself at night, instead of sleeping, making and listening to wave after wave of those rhythmical sentences. But I do manage to sleep, it seems, after an intense writing session—it might be only ten minutes long, but if I have given myself completely to those inner rhythms and managed to embody those rhythms in words on the page, or even if I've failed but have rocked into that spell beyond habit and dailiness, I sometimes sleep soundly, soundlessly, for several hours.

Could it be, then, that the tide of nocturnal sentences I've wanted to dam up is the main source of poetry itself in me? Is this sentence activity my "dumb music," my enrapturer, my inspirer, my harmonizer? Should I be grateful for such sleeplessness? Did Vince Lombardi ever fall asleep on the way to a football game? I think, at this point, I should accept my situation as it is, and should not want to know much more about it. Yes, it would probably be best if my human daylight mind remained less suspicious of the activity than of that dangerous rationality in me that would like to silence my perpetual motion syllable-wheel—*Leonardo DaVinci, Vince Lombardi, Leonardo DaVinci, Vince Lombardi*—turning much of the night at ocean's edge.

Genius

A passage in Emerson's "The Poet" shows the writer the way past being stopped, being fixed, being anxious with unfulfillment. His penultimate paragraph opens: "Doubt not, O Poet, but persist. Say, 'It is in me, and shall out.' Stand there, baulked and dumb, stuttering and stammering, hissed and hooted, stand and strive, until, at last, rage draw out of thee that *dream*-power which every night shows thee is thine own; a power transcending all limit and privacy, and by virtue of which a man is the conductor of the whole river of electricity. Nothing walks, or creeps, or grows, or exists, which must not in turn arise and walk before him as exponent of his meaning. Comes he to that power, his genius is no longer exhaustible."

What power is it then, which, having come into it, we may never exhaust our genius? *Dream*-power, he emphasizes. A *dream*-power finally drawn out of us by "rage," he insists. It is as though he is castigating himself for his own inertia when he has had the cosmic lesson inside himself all the time. Emerson charges the poet to rage his way by way of dream into "the whole river of electricity" wherein our meanings are as voluminous as molecules of water.

How, where, when may we conduct & fuse with this river electric? When we write. In a letter to his brother Charles sent about fifteen years before "The Poet," young Emerson urges Charles to seek "the true image of the soul in the work of the pen." He is essentially not talking about the finished products here—sermons, poems, editorials, essays—but about the meditative act of writing itself. As the pen moves across paper, the writer in semi-trance conducting & fusing with the river of electricity as though in a state of dream, soul may image itself not necessarily in his argument but in the rhythms of his syllables, his phrases, his sentences. Nothing to be fixed. Fluidity. The electrical current of brain & heart rhythming the Oversoul which is not only invoked but in fact *created* by the work of the pen. Come to this realization, this ultimate activity, our genius is not exhaustible. . . .

Mush

A creature the researchers call a "dandelion" is found growing on the lips of a sea-floor vent. Such a beautiful golden uncatalogued myriad-petaled miraculous little plant-animal, as we can see by way of our camera eye down below.

Now we have plucked it with steel fingers, reeled it to surface, and placed it in a glass bowl. But here, in this rational light and pressure, layer after layer its petals and then its heart disintegrate.

Old Sam Peabody

An April hour ago I found a dead bird, its head wedged tightly into the V of a branch of redtwig dogwood at the back of this acre.

I have it in front of me as I write. It has probably been dead for only a few minutes—it's warm and still soft. It's a sparrow of some kind, but with a streak of white down the center of its crown, and with yellow eyebrows, these too becoming streaks of white alongside its head. The rest of its body is rendered in several shades of brown, from dark chestnut to light beige, but in such intricate overlapping arrangements that my probing has already disrupted its featherflow.

The top half of its beak gleams with a dark brown coating that I can easily cut into with my nail. What is this cuticle-like substance? I am only wise enough to know that I am almost entirely stupid about this bird. If I cut through its ribs, could I find and identify its heart? I don't know if a mate mourns for it at this time of the year. I don't know what its nest would look like, or what color or colors its eggs would be. . . .

In *The Lives of a Cell*, Lewis Thomas asks for a moratorium on nuclear apocalypse for at least ten years while mankind tries to find out everything there is to know about at least one living thing on this whole planet. He has a simple creature in mind for study, a protozoan, *Myxotrichia paradoxa*, which lives in the digestive tract of an Australian termite. He tells us a few things about Myx's world, for example that "The flagellae that beat in synchrony to propel mixotrichia with such directness turn out, on closer scrutiny with the electron microscope, not to be flagellae at all. They are outsiders, in to help with the business: fully formed, perfect spirochetes that have attached themselves at regularly spaced intervals all over the surface of the protozoan." Imagine: without these tiny oarsmen, and other even tinier organisms working together in Myx's bailiwick within the termite, wood could not be broken down into loam. Thomas predicts that after ten years of ingesting all information gathered by the best minds in the world with the best technology, the super computer will respond: "Request more data. . . . Do not fire.". . .

I've found a color-plate in my Peterson. My visitor is/was a mature white-throated sparrow. Now I see the patch of white under its beak, and see that it has the unstreaked breast Peterson calls for. He says it has a striped black and white crown, but no, this one's crown is white and the deepest chestnut I have ever seen, almost black but not black, not quite black.

My white-throat preferred the spruce belt's brushy edges and thickets. He sang "several clear, pensive whistles easily imitated," or opened with one or two clear notes and followed "with three quavering notes on a different pitch. New Englanders interpret it as 'Old Sam Peabody, Peabody,' and call the singer the Peabody Bird." As Thomas helps us imagine Myx's spirochete-power, Peterson helps us dream our way back to Old Sam Peabody himself: we can see that long-nosed wit in his red mackinaw shuffling around his New Hampshire farm. Remember the time Old Sam was boiling maple sap and decided to let his two dogs in to watch and a squirrel happened to . . . Why, Sam's Concord neighbors had to . . .

The odorless essence of white-throat is on the morning. I spread the bird's beautiful wings and count its twelve tail-feathers. I think to get out my magnifying glass. But suddenly I realize that, for now, I don't want to know any more. I have something in me that the white-throat no longer has.

Moving north about twelve miles a day, the spring is here again. Nobody knows how this came to be. We do not know what we are. We know *that* we are, and during at least our most lucid moments this is miracle enough to stagger and sustain us. I want to write of this in me, whatever happens, all the way to the end of the world.

Pickerel

Usually, beginning to remember one of my dreams, I'll ask: Did this happen or did that happen? Was it this way or was it that way? But I have just had a very simple and clear and convincing dream; at least for now, I remember all I need to know about it.

In this dream I am not at all confused. I am sixteen, but at the same time as old as I am now. I am with Karen, my first love, walking toward a wood, and at the same time she is not with me, but with others, and watching me. After a while—and, at the same time, right away—I punt a soccer ball.

The idea, I know, is to punt it alongside the dark wood to my right, to keep it in the open field in front of me, of us. This way, I will win a scholarship. In the dream, simultaneously, I both know this and do not know it.

I boom the ball. It's a high kick, curves toward the wood, into the wood. I both regret and do not regret the kick, which I follow into the wood, neither with the others nor apart from them. Deeper in the trees, I look down into a pond, see myself as I was/as I am, and walk away. The ball I am looking for is now a golf ball. It is not that the soccer ball became a golf ball. It is that in the world of this unifying dream, golf ball and soccer ball are the same. My past and my present are the same. My innocence and my experience are the same. There are no ifs, ors, or buts here, as there are in my conscious life (where descriptions by way of opposites, in fact, can be trite and boring), no interruption as there is in even this resolute sentence.

An old man is sitting at a table in the wood selling antiques and golf balls. I know he will become my teacher, and, at the same time in this dream he has been my teacher for many years. "What do you have today?" I ask him. "Same as yesterday," he says. At this point, the dream disappears, but, of course, doesn't, and is still with me. . . .

When I am "awake," everything is split: two brains, going or not-going, having Karen and not having Karen, the living and the dead, winter and summer, gases and solids, the mental life and the physical life, darkness and light, women and men, criminal and victim, anguish and joy, history and future, confusion and clarity. But I realize that within this stunning dream of mine was a rounded revelation (so many of my dreams are angles and fragments) of the nature of the universe, and that right now, despite everything else on my mind from my paycheck to the apocalyptic two-volume 1988 Environmental Protection Agency draft report to Congress called "The Potential Effects of Global Climate Change on the United States"—all species, everything alive, it seems to me, is endangered—I can start smiling. It is obvious to me and beyond merely wishful thinking that my deepest self has always known Oneness, or I could not have dreamt it so convincingly. In an 1857 journal entry Emerson says, "For the soul in dreams has a subtle synthetic power which it will not exert under the sharp eyes of day."

But we have only words as we try to recount intimations of the great unity. I've tried here to express a dream that was the thing itself. Can an essay or poem, by way of vivid leaps and jolts and/or stream of mind upon silence embody and communicate such an experience? To try to suggest cosmic seamlessness mystics—Native American and Christian and Buddhist (if there is such a thing as a Buddhist mystic)—have spoken in oxymorons, square circles and cold fires and dry tears and snow blossoms. The great Zen poets help us realize *wholeness*: a dragonfly's motionless speed, the flow of rock and skylark, a frog's fusion with water, the politics of candles and sparrow-monks. I think of a Lucien Stryk translation of Basho: "Moon-daubed bush-clover—/ssh, in the next room/snoring prostitutes."

Poetry, in its relationship to Being, is something like the relationship between Thoreau's pickerel and their pond. He describes them as "the animalized *nuclei* or crystals of the Walden water." And how miraculous it is that we have them: "It is surprising that they are caught here,—and that in this deep and capacious spring, far beneath the rattling teams and chaises and tinkling sleighs that travel the Walden road, this great gold and emerald fish swims." And how priceless, *hors commerce*: "I never chanced to see its kind in any market; it would be the cynosure of all eyes there." And how, after this embodiment, we are connected with them to the great sea: "Easily, with a few convulsive quirks, they give up their watery ghosts, like a mortal translated before his time to the thin air of heaven."

Milkweed swim in the margins of my western New York State acre. One summer day, I noticed the first slight tinge of a second color in their buds and wrote this poem, called "Ensoulment":

> Before mid-summer,
> only hard green
> in the milkweed buds,
>
> but now, as here,
> the first faint mauve light
> does appear
>
> from under sepals:
> even underground,
> how long had it been there? When were
>
> such petals
> ever dead? How could it
> not always have been there?

As did my dream, this poem, this time by way of rhetorical questions, seems able to conceive of Oneness. There is a mauve light here which does not come into being at any one millisecond during the summer, but always *is*, underground or in that place which is at once nowhere and everywhere. And my general sense of the "process" of writing is this: I wrote that poem, in moments of meditation and semi-trance, to remind my conscious self of what my deeper self (Walt Whitman's "me myself") knows to be true. Did Walt, by the way, achieve *satori* before or during the composition of those masterpieces of wholeness "Song of Myself" and "To Think of Time" and "The Sleepers" woven, without titles, into the first edition of the *Leaves*? Yes.

There is an "imperishable quiet at the heart of form," Theodore Roethke says. A poem can achieve this tremulous balance, and can be during its writing an aide for the writer, during its reading an aide for the reader, in reaching this. I emphasize the "during"—we *do* surface and begin to talk/buy/dissect/classify/explain. Still, if we remain faithful to that quiet . . .

One of environmentalist Barry Commoner's four fundamental laws of ecology—these hold true at once within earthly and cosmic spheres, tangibly and spiritually, I believe—is that "Everything must go somewhere." There are transformations, but nothing goes away. No ends, no beginnings. Thoreau says that the pickerel are "watery ghosts" that are "translated."

When I was a boy, I fished a pond that fed into Lake Ronkonkoma on Long Island. We could catch catfish, sunnies, perch, an occasional bass but never the beautiful elusive pickerel that disdained our bait. But one late afternoon I saw two of them suspended in the shadow of my head under lily pads four or five feet from shore. (There is a stillness inside stillness, and they were so elementally and electrically still that they still hover in my mind like words I am not yet quite able to say.) I cast worms in front of them—they did not blink or flinch or show the slightest interest. Then, because I was/am a murderer and a creator, I dropped a hook over one's back, and snagged it, pulled it to shore, injured or killed it—I don't remember. But, despite me, that earlier image of the two pickerel abides, imperishable, the place of poetry before and beyond the clever and the lethal, abides within the dimension that moment-by-moment spawns the galaxies, that spawns my dream of wholeness in which there is a pond in which, I am sometimes certain, the pickerel live, and will.

Fish

The legend of the lunker lurking in a particular pool, bass in a deep place beneath a tangle of logs at the base of a waterfall, catfish at the riverbend where the current has scooped out a cave, trout beneath a shelf of shale. The fish is old, of course, is seen at most a few times a year, has broken lines, carries enough lures in its lip to stock a store.

Those who go after it do not want to land it, even as they do—supper would be a mess of shadows. In water, alive, the fish is like a word, one of those words that is still a poem, a story. . . .

Waiting there for me now, again, in electrical stillness, a pickerel under the lily pads in a creek feeding into Lake Ronkonkoma.

The Father of My Country

I stood up in old Nesconset school with the rest of my classmates—
I was seven, eight, nine, ten—my hand over my heart. I faced the front
of the room where, above the blackboard, between engravings of The
Father of Our Country on one side and The Pilgrims at Thanksgiving
Dinner with the Indians on the other, a 48-starred flag presided over our
classroom. The day's leader began the chant, the rest of us picking it up
after five or six syllables. In this way, with this communal activity, we
began our day. For years I chanted that rote chant—it could as well have
been in Swahili or in tongues: ". . . and to the republic for Richard
Stands." Richard owes me something now, I think, at least one para-
bolic paragraph after all those years I went on pledging the republic to
him.

The End

In high school I won a football in a raffle. Katie Lee, sexy cheerleader, pushed it to me reluctantly Monday morning in Latin.

Painfully shy and feeling inferior, I hadn't attended the pep rally where "Stone" Cummings, team captain, had drawn my name from a trophy and asked, "Anybody know this Billy Hymen or whoever he is?"

Years later, I could order a meal from a waitress without blushing or becoming tongue-tied. I could kiss the woman who would become my wife and who would one day find, in a box of high school papers and yearbooks, a football signed by "Block" Patterson, "Snake" Lewis, "Zombie" Marko, "Bird" Leonard, and the Stone man himself.

That autumn of 1955 Stone and his teammates had battered the opposition into submission. Thirty years later, I propped the football on my mantle and looked at it in safety. . . . "The name of it is Time," says Robert Penn Warren in the last section of *Audubon: A Vision.* "But you must not pronounce its name.". . .

Today, my intuitive twenty-year-old daughter took it down and flipped me a lateral across our living room. We ran outside for passes and punts. It was about time. I wonder where all those tough guys are now as my prize begins its postponed history of scrapes, lumps, protruding bladder, loose laces, its names spiralling all the way from high school and turning end over end to the end.

Evergreen

This evening I saw Mrs. Louis, whose husband died just a week ago, walk out across her back lawn to the blue spruce—her "feeder-tree" she calls it—under which she's always scattered birdseed and into which she's always tied cubes of suet for nuthatches and chickadees. She walked slowly around the tree once, twice, then began tying something into it.

I walked halfway across my back lawn to where I could stand hidden behind lilacs. What she'd tied to the spruce branch gleamed. It seemed to be a silver or gold bracelet.

Mrs. Louis kept doing whatever it was she was doing. Objects glittered in the branches. It took me a while to realize she was tying her jewelry to the tree, piece after piece, diamond rings and pearl necklaces, earrings, wristwatches.

Later, after she'd gone inside and had shut off her lights, I visited the tree, walked around it in starshine and moonlight. I didn't count, but there must have been fifty pieces of jewelry in the tree. . . .

In the morning, I'll have to read this situation more clearly, will have to do something, but what? For now, that evergreen, her poem, is all that Mrs. Louis can do to celebrate her grief.

Notes Toward a Note on "Notes Toward"

I like the phrase "notes toward."

It is humble, suggesting jottings. Nothing at stake here. Brainstorming for possibilities. Half a chance the writing will all come to nothing consequential, that the notes will just be thrown away, or filed.

It is hopeful. Maybe, just maybe the leaves & twigs will become branches supported by a trunk & root system in viable soil. To switch metaphors the way notes give license to switch, maybe the gnats will pester the burro into at least braying.

It is realistic. What else is even a great novel (*Moby Dick*) or poem ("Song of Myself") but "notes toward" wholeness & completion? If one book could say it all, we wouldn't have so many. Even all the holy scriptures together are notes toward the saying that will be said, probably wordlessly, at the instant of our eventual revelation. The critic Stephen E. Whicher says of Emerson that "One gradually comes to realize that all his work is like one great essay, whose subject is 'Man Thinking'."

I'm thinking of a man who has been up all night. He is sitting by himself in a fast food place god knows where. He is writing in a blank book. I think he's retired. I think this is his first such blank book—he must have bought it on impulse. I think he's been writing in it for only a few weeks. He sips coffee, puts his cup down, opens this notebook, gazes up, writes a phrase or sentence, closes this book again, picks up his coffee again, sips. . . .

He is making notes toward thoughts & feelings which exist in him in a musical matrix but which seem to him conflicted, incoherent, cacophonous. After making an entry, however, he almost always feels better, but for no good reason he can think of.

All his entries, though he does not think of it in this way, are notes from a life come to grief, & a life that will come *through* grief. For now, after two more sentences, he's finished: *May she rest in peace. What's left for me now but this?*

The Wool

Life is not a dream. We can't easily or without penalties escape from it. We wake up into it again every morning, wherever we've been, and closer, it may be, to something we fear: that last day which draws closer to us each day. Life's unity, its continuousness—we wake in the same body and consciousness—is itself amazing and daunting. Why in the variegated timelessness of sleep do not all our atoms scatter into other vast systems of embodiment and dream? We are so deeply rooted here, or seem to be.

Our years, though, do slide by like a river under a stilted house in which we sleep, "wake," sleep again. Logs bump the stilts. Emerson thought it the sorriest mark of our condition that experience does not hook us so that we stay hooked. He lamented the "evanescence and lubricity" of time. He felt helpless even in holding to his grief over the death of his son. (And three years after the death of his daughter, William Wordsworth, forgetting for a moment she is dead, turns to share a moment of "transport" with her, then wonders "Through what power, / Even for the least division of an hour, / Have I been so beguiled as to be blind / To my most grievous loss!") But this constitutional lubricity is our defense against nihilism, it seems, and might itself indicate the existence of that whole life into which we will flow when our timebound earthly house falls into the river.

Hold me here, poem, for a little while, both in this identity, this consciousness, and in that afterworld of eternity my heart intimates and desires. Even as I feel the river rising, thrumming the stilts, hold me here for now. Lyric poem, let there be no division in you, but spellbound duration; let it seem that you are spoken in an instant in me, as much all-of-a-piece as was the wool of a sheep shorn by neighbor Wenzel when I was a boy.

The Wool

Wenzel upends the sheep gently,
kneels to it, knees it still,
careful to console it as he holds it.

I hear electric whirr under
the sheep's plaintive bleating,
Wenzel shearing first its rump, then

brisket and neck, down
shoulders to belly, smoothly, then
the left side and then the right. . . .

I lift this full fleece away,
this harvest without death,
the shorn sheep rising, returning

to fold, frightened, maybe chilled,
but closer to its inner light,
and no worse off for its gift.

Yourself be the sacrament, lyric poem, all that we have ever been, lost
song for a moment found, our holiest book unfolding, the soul finding
its melodic fold and welcoming itself home.

Sheep This Evening

I live on a star
moving at great speed,
directionless toward Virgo,

but Wenzel's sheep this evening,
themselves their own cosmos,
poised in dumbness,
graze, nip

the growing grass short,
while I gaze Virgo,
its bright star Spica, space
I pray to curve from,

as the animals' world persists,
their bleat-musics,
green-black grass
within the light's years.

Lord, preserve
such fields, and I would be
among them when all matter
disappears, the bodiless

sheep one evening not surprised,
their eyes revolving, light recording
that I've returned.

A Note on Romanticism

Reading my poem "Lord Dragonfly" to about a hundred prisoners at Attica some years ago, I got to section xvii. My poem begins as my speaker wonders where the dead are, and in this section, with one ecstatic rhetorical question, he demolishes the whole idea of the dark night of the soul and of the abyss. I spoke the section's two lines: "With trees overhead, / where is the void?" Immediately a prisoner shouted, "Over the trees."

Castaneda

I walked up to Carlos Castaneda at the Boston Grayhound Bus Station. I asked him, "Are you here or in Mexico?"

"I travel very fast," he said.

Near us, a man dropped three quarters into a slot, opened a locker, stuffed in a suitcase and two dufflebags. He removed the key and hurried off.

"Where's your luggage?" I asked Carlos.

"I travel very light," he said.

I remembered that his name meant "chestnut grove" in Spanish. "Where has the American chestnut tree gone, Carlos?"

"They are on the horizon," he said.

A voice sputtered over the station loudspeaker, something about when to board where to get someplace.

"What are you doing here, anyway?" I asked the chestnut sapling growing beside me?

Floor tiles cracked, leaves blocked the fluorescent ceiling lights.

My bus followed a path through a chestnut forest. Carlitos was driving. Windwaves moved through the trees' branches above us.

"This is wherever we were when we were here before," he said.

"Where's here?" I said.

"Yes," he said.

All this night we drove under chestnut branches for me to arrive here at this time now.

Translation Ambush

In *The Lance and the Shield: The Life and Times of Sitting Bull* Robert M. Utley describes the recollection of a young Lakota named Standing Bear who was in the audience in Philadelphia in 1884 when Sitting Bull made a speech. The holy man and warrior, said Standing Bear, spoke about "the end of fighting and the need for the children to be educated. He and his friends, the chief concluded, were on their way to Washington to shake hands with the Great Father and talk about peace."

A white man rose to translate Sitting Bull's oration. The man crafted "a lurid rendition of the Little Bighorn, complete with warriors springing from ambush to wipe out all of Custer's soldiers."

Let's get the show on the road. Buffalo Bill Cody is waiting in the wings to travel with Sitting Bull. It's a shame Crazy Horse was murdered in 1877—he'd have been a great attraction—but let's make some money. Let's send these city-folk home with something to dream about besides how their geraniums are blooming on their porches and fire escapes. With much deceit and guile, the translator "translated" what he heard by the light of who he was. Let's give Sitting Bull two bucks for his autographed picture & get this translation, this souvenir book into print in a hurry.

Sycamore & Ash

If the sycamore on my front lawn were able to speak, & did, I would not understand.

I would not understand this sycamore speech not because all the world's translators could not help me, not because of a failure of translation, but because I would be, as I am so far in my common life, unable to find anything that would translate into speech itself. The sycamore's would be pure presence, the natural act of soul undivided from itself, a wholeness of essence, a fused utterance, while I attempted, in effect, to find a meaningful cipher for the vowel of a single leaf. A sycamore sheds bark as I shed hair & skin, is a creature of soil & water & sunlight as I am, but if it spoke I would be in the aura of speech speaking, & my ego, which insists on equivalents & rational mind, would be shocked & baffled.

At the same time, the sycamore does communicate, of course. Wind vibrates its leaves, its branches rub together, it makes sounds, yes, but I mean something else. Its innate speech is one of moving forms & colors; its lines coalesce, its resemblances dissipate & rearrange, its dumb music is at once opening theme, transitional passage, & melody, if I could hear, dear god that speaks plants & weather & animals & human beings such as myself, help me to hear this shifting meditation of visible matter, this companion.

In related prayer, I almost begin to hear, again, in this present, a thirty-year-old poem of mine, another tree, "The Eternal Ash":

> By early August, the mountain ash's each limb
> hangs heavy, its berry clusters
> already tinged orange and bending its body
> almost to breaking. The ash bears,
>
> and will, this light, this weight.
> Even at night under the frost stars, each berry
> deepens into the ripe flame
> autumn means for it to be,

yes, but to know one thing, but know it:
the lord of the whole tree, in time,
unchanged, its changes mine, delusion;
knowing, now, the mystical winter blossom. . . .

Which August is this, anyway?—this windless
poise of clusters that never fall, but will,
within the living tree that withers, while
ashlight drifts to the earth, petal by petal.

Open Letter to the SUNY Brockport College Community

(Autumn 1988)

At our last Department of English meeting, my friends and I discussed our curriculum. We wondered, in part, if we were keeping up with many new ways of reading literature—postmodern approaches including poststructuralism deconstruction, narratology (a word new to me), etc. We spoke about our departmental mission, and the mission of our College. As I often do, I was drifting in and out of the talk, hearing the Hartwell Hall bells, breathing the slant of end-of-summer light, calling up scenes from my student days at Brockport in the '50s, thinking about the young people in my classes this semester and wondering how I could help them find their ways as some of my teachers helped me find mine.

Then, after an hour or so as our discussion became more and more convoluted and technical, I found myself saying something that apparently had been building up in me for a long time, only appearing, in understated ways, in my poems and stories. I said that I read much literature on our environment. I said, given our current direction, it's hard for me to conceive that human life will exist on this planet a hundred years from now. "What if this is true?" I asked. I wondered what *this* should do to our sense of our curriculum, this impending extinction of mankind.

I've become convinced that this very real possibility is the one thing that we cannot, no matter how hard we try, concentrate on, much less imagine. In one of his poems James Dickey says, "Lord, let me die, / but not die / out." I find myself, usually, at ease about growing old and about dying. I've already had, at forty-seven, a rich and lucky life. But to dwell on the possibility that we could "die out," that our grandchildren and theirs for countless generations would not people this planet, would not smell grass, fall in love with one another, watch leaves ramify, see clouds or waves sail and crest—this is something that makes us more than heartsick. It threatens our sanity. If it is true that within a hundred years we will all die out . . . But, no, we can't concentrate on this possibility, can't imagine our beloved earth within a silence devoid of human presence. "Faith is the antiseptic of the soul," Whitman says. "It pervades the common people [whom Walt loves and among whom I count myself] and preserves them . . . they never give up believing and expecting and trusting."

This brief letter to you is not the place for me to muster in a scholarly way my arguments and evidence—the thousand chemicals found in the fat of a dying population of seals, our weakened and blight-stricken forests, our acid-dead lakes, dioxin dumps on the Niagara River that could kill every living thing in and around the Great Lakes a thousand times over, the daily destruction of various species we've not even had time to study, the million acres of American farmland lost to asphalt each year, Bangladesh disappearing because of deforestation in China, our oceans' plankton beds diminishing in volume and ability to provide oxygen, ozone holes in our atmosphere, the poisoning of our land and food, inundation of the environment with garbage and sludge and insoluble nuclear waste. We all read about (and contribute to) these catastrophes. But if you are like me, the message doesn't quite penetrate. Emily Dickinson writes, "A Thought went up my mind today— / That I have had before— / But did not finish—some way back— / I could not fix the Year—" Will we get used to the warnings until we're bored, or will we, with all the intensity we can call up in ourselves, keep this precariousness of our existence on earth in mind? My mind finds many ways to protect itself, to distract my deeper self from what seems to me the obvious possibility that nobody will be alive in Brockport, or in the United States, or anywhere, in 2088, before which time, surely, we will *not* locate and be able to reach another habitable planet to ruin. We are here, or we are nowhere, at least in body.

Our minds will create counter-arguments to ecological awareness. We might tell ourselves, for example, that if we pay too-close attention to the possibility of extinction, joy will go out of our lives. Yes, but this might be our necessary burden now, for in a hundred years, maybe, there will be *no* life and *no* joy on earth. Our minds will find a hundred intricate ways to distract attention from what, it seems to me, must be the central thing we must be thinking about. All deep thought is deflected to the Buffalo Bills (I'm a fan), to Harlequin romances (I'm not a fan), to advertising that keeps selling us things we don't need. The one thing we must all be thinking about seethes in the unconscious, if anywhere. You will leave this letter behind, as I will, and get on with your life as you have been living it, as I will. (Our administration, our Faculty Senate, our student body, our Brockport Village Board will not hold emergency meetings.) But what if it is true that within a hundred years . . . ?

A century is only a human lifetime or two. I've dozens of books in my study that are more than a hundred years old, one going back to 1518—the centuries since are only a blink in time.

I'm thinking about us as a college community, and I suppose I'm trying to edge toward only one suggestion here, a suggestion of awareness: that our first realization should be—whatever we administer, whatever we teach, whatever we study—that if we do not concentrate on our approaching ecological nightmare (ecology: the wisdom of earthly relations), we have no future. Except insofar as our physical education and recreation programs can come to serve this end, they will not matter in the least. Except insofar as literature and composition can come to serve this end, they will not matter in the least. Except insofar as the study of history, or political science, or business, or dance, or philosophy, or mathematics, or physics, or computer science first serve this end, these disciplines will not matter, will have proved to be worthless distractions, and will in a hundred years not exist. Insofar as our multi-cultural thrust at Brockport does not serve this end, it will not matter, for in a hundred years there will be no cultures at all. (I feel this not as a narrowing down wherever we administer and teach and study, but as an opening up into metaphor that will *integrate* our curriculums: the dance, e.g., has to do with the *healthy* body in time and space; physics with matters of *energy* and force; agriculture with what Wendell Berry calls "kindly use" of the land, with *stewardship* for the future; poetry with the discovery of balances and intricate relationships among all its elements; etc.)

Thoreau tells us that he knows "of no more encouraging fact than the unquestionable ability of man to elevate his life by a conscious endeavor." He also says that there are a thousand hacking at the branches of problems to one who is striking at the root. I have very strong feelings about the roots of the problems—in me, in you, in the assumptions of our society and economy—that are funneling us toward non-existence, but this is not the place for me to try to discuss these. This letter is hacking away in the branches only to say that 1/ on our current course, the death of the planet is at hand in the near future; 2/ we need to focus the black light of this thought within our minds, and adjust our curriculums, our studies, our lives, our "conscious endeavor(s)" toward awareness, the first step toward making a difference. We might become the first community in the country, in the world, to wake from our daily blur and begin to articulate and face that awful possibility to which we've so far not even been able to pay attention.

The Host: An Address to the Faculty at SUNY Brockport

(December 5, 1988)

Two hours from now it will seem unreal to me that I was here talking to you about *this*. The sense of unreality I have / we have when considering these matters is part of the problem, surely.

Apparently, I'd been trying to slant away from what needs to reach surface in me. I'd been staying busy, teaching and reading and writing, when all at once I felt I had to send that "Open Letter" to which so many of you responded. Probably because of what we sense we are coming to, we have all been afraid, maybe, that there would come a point when we could not just go on with what we were doing, not in the same old way, with the same old consciousness. I haven't wanted this to disrupt my life from here on in. But why shouldn't it? We have to be strong about our terrible anxiety, whatever form it takes, strong together. Poet Richard Wilbur wrote me, in part, "You're right, it does threaten our sanity that so many of us, judging the ecological and nuclear situations to be out of hand, are in a state of covert fear and near despair." He mentions a necessary state of "reasonable dread."

Thanks to Congressman John LaFalce's office I've gotten hold of and have been reading the Environmental Protection Agency's recent two-volume draft report to Congress called "The Potential Effects of Global Climate Change on the United States." It says that we on this planet "because of past greenhouse gas emissions" are, over the next century, "committed to" a rise in temperature of 3-8 degrees. It seems to me—do we have to be struck over the head with a hammer?—that this in itself will probably be catastrophic in myriad ways, but as you know we've generaly had a tendency to underestimate the severity of environmental problems, and many of us believe the temperature rise will be higher. Just think of Russia and China fast becoming western-style consumer societies (several new Kentucky Fried Chickens are going up in Peking because of the success of their pilot franchise there this past year); think of the proliferation of asphalt and automobiles and acid rain industries.

94

Polar ice caps will melt, and ocean levels will rise between 20 inches and 6 feet, the EPA says. At a cost of billions, we could attempt to dike off coastal areas, but we would still lose 4,000 to 10,000 square miles of coast. We'll lose more. Tree lines will shift, if they have time to and if soils prove hospitable, and forests will die out, the EPA admits. Surely, we can anticipate confusion and chaos in farm belts whose weathers will not sustain crops. There will be increased demands for electrical and other power as the earth gets hotter and hotter, as it becomes more and more industrialized, as we achieve more and more "progress," more and more "development."

There are other possible scenarios. Some argue that the "greenhouse effect" will create a cloud cover that will quickly *cool* the earth, bringing on an ice-age within decades. In any case, the general science of the problem—carbon dioxide and other greenhouse gases including methane trapping heat—is not an issue. And it is beyond dispute that carbon dioxide levels and temperature are rising. Most scientists expect a *doubling* of carbon dioxide levels by the 2030s. The long-term effects are not absolutely certain, but, as a reviewer of several books on global climate has recently said in *The New York Review of Books,* "The situation, then, is one of scattered dissent amid general scientific consensus on these matters." And the general scientific consensus now is that we are in grave trouble, to say the least.

Before I leave the EPA summary report, listen to just a few of its sentences. "Strategies to reverse such impacts on natural ecosystems are not currently available." "If current trends continue, it is likely that climate may change too quickly for many natural systems to adapt." "Forest declines may be visible in as little as a few decades.... Once this process starts, major dieback may occur rapidly." And listen to the wishful thinking that however gives way to fear when the report tries to suggest solutions: "Farmers may also switch to more heat- and drought-resistant crop varieties, plant two crops during a growing season, and plant and harvest earlier. Whether these adjustments would compensate for climate change depends on a number of factors including the severity of the climate change." Sometimes the report, its language and logic, seems spoken by some kind of Big Brother machine: "If people acclimatize by using air-conditioning, changing workplace habit, and altering the construction of homes and cities, the impact on summer mortality rates may be substantially reduced. . . . The relationship between pollution episodes and weather events on mortality is unknown. Further investigations currently under way may provide additional insights into these causes of death." My general feeling about the EPA report is that its well-meaning writers are trying to stave off panic. A language of reason collides with frightening facts and projections. How have they slept? How have they stayed sane? Reading the report, I kept thinking of Arthur Miller's stage directions in *Death of a Salesman:* "an air of the dream clings to the place." That play is about a fearful dream. The EPA report of our future is fearful. But it is not a dream.

I must trust myself in this. I know what I know. When I was a boy I waded Long Island ponds and *knew.* I had a sense of presence, something indwelling in the water and the trees and the creatures of the ponds. From nature, I knew / I know I am a spiritual being. As Walt Whitman says, I know I am not contained only between hat and shoes. But those places that sustained me physically and spiritually, that sustain me now even in my memories of them, are asphalt or lurid lawns that seep the poisons poured on them. I came to Brockport as a sixteen-year-old student. I now drive my car where I once walked through woods. I shop on land where I once played golf.

We know, or should know, what a healthy terrarium is, what a healthy aquarium is, and how they can so easily be thrown off balance. We must trust ourselves in this: surely we know that the way we are going we will not survive, the human race will not continue, beyond a hundred years, give or take a decade or three. Tree and fish diebacks are becoming human diebacks. We are constricting ourselves toward breathlessness. Every second we sit here, every second we sleep an area of tropical forest the size of a football field is being slashed and burned, its mysterious ecosystems turned to carbon dioxide, its fragile soils, in the main, to be depleted or washed away in a few seasons. . . .

But these are just words, and I know of this extinction, usually, only with my mind. Only for a few seconds a day do I truly *imagine* our race coming to a close. My blood rushes to my organs, I go cold, and my mind shuts itself off.

I try to focus on this bodily reaction. It may be that the one thing we are physiologically unable, *unable* to think about is this coming death. It is not that we do not want to be aware of this, maybe. It is that we cannot become aware of it, cannot imagine it, cannot imagine these streets, this whole village and county and region and continent empty of us. To *imagine*, to bring this into a heart-mind conjunctioning—this is what I have been trying to jolt myself toward. But there is danger in imagining this, short-circuit and flame in the mind. Emily Dickinson says, "The brain within its groove / Runs evenly and true / But let a splinter swerve / Twere easier for you / To put a current back / When floods have slit the hills . . ." Floods *will* slit our hills and brainfolds.

Imagine, a hundred years from now—and several people who responded to my letter said that they thought it would be sooner—no human beings on earth. If this is what is going to happen, if it is even *possible* that this is going to happen, then everything else that we are thinking about, dealing with, is just distracting us. All human history, in these terms, will have become nothingness, an absence, and our music, our art, our wars, our presidents, our religions, our bodies of laws, our slave or immigrant or Native American ancestors, our great universities, our cities and cathedrals, all the beloved dead of all our studies will all be as if they had never existed. What will the abortion issue matter, really, if in a hundred years no one is alive on the planet. The budget deficit? The struggle by women and minorities for equal rights? The question of trade agreements between the U.S. and Canada? The Israeli-Arab conflict? What's the difference, except regarding the temporary question of comfort or discomfort or slightly longer survival for this group or that group, this country or that country, over the next century or so. In these final and so far unimaginable terms, we as a society seem to approach everything in a superficial, absurdly irrelevant way. It may be that we are going to die out, die out soon and absolutely. Imagine, some children born today may be there at the end.

Some will say that these are scare tactics, that such an argument serves only to deflect attention from the civil rights struggle, from the disappearing family farm, from AIDS research, from laser research, from the space program, from funding of the arts, from this or that cause. But if we go on the way we have, there will be no causes at all a hundred years from now. If you say I'm an alarmist, I say that the necessary evidence is already in, and that you are an obstructionist. Greenpeace research reveals that the Baltic Sea is virtually dead from toxic contaminants, that by the year 2000 not a drop of water will be available in all of Poland for even industrial use. Is it any secret that this poisoning is also occurring in our oceans? Is it any secret that we cannot survive with dead oceans?

But all issues, all our studies and activities can be made central to what must be our first priority, the curriculum integration I spoke of in the "Open Letter."

One person responded anonymously to the letter, scrawling at the bottom of it in purple ink, "no one person can break up a whirlwind by jumping off a cliff into the middle of it. Relax, perhaps we will be replaced by a wiser species. At least we were given a chance. Let's celebrate opportunity." What to make of this, this resignation to give up the world so easily? Even if the writer is sure of another one (as I sometimes am), do we not love this world of rabbits and black-capped chickadees, of sunflowers and cabbages and spring hyacinths, of one another? . . . (Maybe not—maybe the dire truth is that we don't, and that because we don't we cherish a deathwish. If this is true, we must recognize and exorcise this, too, during our educations.)

Another person responded to my letter by writing, "We are natural creatures. Therefore what we do is natural. If we tear down a forest and pave the place where once it stood, that is natural." You can hear where this inexorable (but maybe false) logic takes us—to the resignation to whirlwind again. I want to say *no* to this. I want to hold to the faith that our destruction of ourselves is *not* natural, that stupidity and short-sightedness need not be our unavoidable condition and fate. Whitman says he is the poet of good and evil. He says he grafts the good onto himself and translates the evil into a new tongue. Maybe it would be best for the human enterprise if we assumed that our stupidity and selfishness and short-sightedness were curable aberrations, that we could translate them into new tongues. The same respondent says there is "nothing to indicate everlasting existence of us or any other creature." Maybe not, but there are areas in China, I understand, that have been farmed by families for thousands of years without loss of soil fertility. Do we in our grandchildren's or great-grandchildren's time have to lose everything? Why not another thousand generations? Who knows what we might discover by then!

Li Po was a Chinese poet who lived a thousand years ago. He referred to our Milky Way as the "cloudy river of the sky." I mention him at the end of my poem called "Brockport, New York: Beginning with 'And'":

as billions of grassblades lose their light.
as maples rise sable-red within the black air,
as years number us further and further away,
as stars course their patterns
and earth flows Li Po's eternal river,
someone will know, and remember,
and be set dreaming,
and will say "and."

I wrote that poem some years ago. I now realize how deeply afraid I've been that no one, in a hundred years, will be alive in this community, or anywhere else, to say "and."

I need of course to do much more thinking, but I've been thinking this: that we should not rush to bring to Brockport experts from outside to explain our excruciating dilemma to us. We need to begin here, with ourselves. (I say this despite a recent editorial in *Greenpeace* that says we have to think beyond René Dubos's "think globally, act locally," that "many problems, such as global limits on marine and atmospheric pollutants, are most quickly and efficiently solved at the level of international agreements and forums.") Maybe this community can wake up to this necessity of imagining, somehow, the possible end of everything human. I'm thinking about a college community, ours, as an ecosystem, one that needs to become healthy, both physically and mentally. We have lost the *margins* that we had, either for physical or intellectual pollution. We are specializing ourselves toward non-existence. I'm thinking about the college and this village and town as a place where we come to imagination together, where we in mind and body strike through to realizations that will naturally flow and translate into action.

A couple of months ago I was entering Hartwell Hall and noticed in a little triangle of grass one of those flags warning that chemicals had been sprayed. And I've seen workers here spraying between the stones around the Special Olympics fountain, and along the curbs at Cooper. Could we not become a pesticide/herbicide-free college, and come to brag about it, even to advertise ourselves as being enlightened enough to stop poisoning ourselves? Is ours a problem in aesthetics, therefore a problem in education? I mean, what makes us believe that a homogeneous lawn of bluegrass or whatever is any more attractive than a *diverse* (and therefore ecologically healthier) lawn of clovers and crabgrasses and dandelions and chicories and milkweed on which monarch butterflies lay their eggs? Are we all crazy? And do these chemicals change from year to year, and build up in our soils until they combine in such complex toxic ways that we are bequeathing to our students and townspeople and ourselves serious illnesses? Are we so oblivious to our approaching doom that intellectually we are giving our students nothing to take into their own lives with them with which they can make a difference in their communities and with their own children and students? Wendell Berry urges that we "Think Little" to begin, and I am thinking about a small but central thing here. Our use of pesticides and herbicides touches on business, on economics, on politics, on nutrition and health, on psychology, on aesthetics and poetry, on sports management, on leisure activities, on our concept of what work itself is. The flag in the tiny triangle of grass behind Hartwell points to a problem we have in educating ourselves and our students and our townspeople.

If, in the face of the nightmare into which we seem to be rushing, we have no immediate answers, we can set an example. We can begin to imagine. Maybe, if our college becomes a place where learning can take place, we will host students in a year or ten years who *will* be able to make a difference around the world. Surely, right now, our curriculum, as is every other curriculum everywhere, is short-sighted, to say the least. And our town is way behind: I saw a report on a recycling program in Wellesley, Massachusetts, on "Good Morning America" that gave me much hope. 75% of the people in Wellesley participate. The town actually raises almost $200,000 a year recycling. Where are our elected town and village officials on this? Where are our business leaders? Where is our recyling program at the college? Where are our grade and high schools? Where am I? So far, nowhere.

To begin with, we should require a course on these matters of all freshmen and transfers. Surely it would be the single most important course we could offer. We have required quantitative skills and communications skills, but do not require the only skills that can save us, ecology skills. The course should state in no uncertain terms that ecological systems are breaking down. The course should exemplify integrated thinking, should sensitize students to insist that because human life is on the edge of extinction, all other of their courses should also bear centrally on final things. The course could be based on Barry Commoner's "Four Laws of Ecology" from his book *The Closing Circle*—these laws have endless ramifications across the sciences-humanities spectrum: 1/ *Everything is connected to everything else*. (Think of Chernobyl and the caribou culture of the Laplanders.) 2/ *Everything must go somewhere*. (Think of industry in the Ohio Valley and the 285 dead lakes in the Adirondacks; think of what repressed anger does to the human body.) 3/ *Nature knows best*. (Think of how you coughed when you first smoked a cigarette, of why a vulture's neck has no feathers, of why nitrate fertilizers are eventually and inevitably ruinous, of ozone and ultraviolet balances and skin cancers.) 4/ *There is no such thing as a free lunch*. (Have you ever heard what cleaning up various nuclear plants will cost us? Do we think we can cut down 2000-year-old redwoods forever?)

I would like to see us develop, in fact, *four* required courses, one a year on each of these interrelated principles. Learning to teach and teaching these courses, and I say this realizing what I'm saying, we could as a whole become the world's worthiest faculty.

Thank you for listening. I'll conclude with a poem called "The Host." I wrote it about ten years ago, no doubt using it to try to face and sublimate my fears. Now, like its main character, it erupts again.

The Host

> In the dying pond,
> under an oilspilled rainbow where
> cement clumped, cans rusted, and slick tires
> glinted their whitewall irises,
> at the edge where liquid congealed,
> a lump of mud shifted.
> I knew what it was,
> and knelt to poke it with a wire
> from the saddest mattress in the world.
>
> Maybe a month out of its rubbery egg
> the young snapper hid,
> or tried to, drew back its head,

but algae-scum outlined its oval shell,
its ridged chine diminished
toward its tail,
and I lifted the turtle
into the air, its jaws open,
its crooked neck unfolding upward.

It twisted, could not reach me.
I found out its soft, small undershell where,
already, a leech lodged
beneath its left hindleg, sucking
some of whatever blood
its host could filter from the pond, its host.
They would grow together, if the snapper lived.
Its yellow eyes insisted it would.
I gave it back to the oil sludge

where it was born, and watched it
bury itself, in time, and disappear. . . .
I'd like to leave it living there,
but churned slime above it blurs, burns,
bursts into black glare, every atom
of chemical water, rust residue, human vomit
shining in deathlight.
The snapper's bleached shell ascends the 21st century,
empty, beyond illusion.

I'd like to refer the reader to two other of my esays on ecology that are not included in *Pig Notes*: "The Green Gate: Memory, Extinction, and the Artist's Imagination," *NCECA Journal*, 11 (1990-91), 22-30; and "Spring Letter to Geof Hewitt," *The New Review*, 1, 1 (May-June 1992), 39-45. An autobiographical essay ("Home," in *Contemporary Authors: Autobiography Series*, ed. Mark Zadrozny, Vol. 9 [Detroit: Gale Research Co., 1989], 31-48), my memoir *With Me Far Away* (Roslyn, N.Y.: The Stone House Press, 1994), and *Pterodactyl Rose: Poems of Ecology* (Saint Louis: Time Being Books, 1991) also center on this theme.

An Open Letter to Mr. Ehrlich's Students

It was raining this morning, and I was thinking about the rain, or maybe I was just day-dreaming. How strange it is, really, that droplets of water form in the sky and fall to earth. This happens where you are around Wingate High in Brooklyn, and where I am here in western New York.

Did you ever have the sudden feeling that your life is a miracle? I mean, how is it possible that we have these bodies of ours? How is it that we're conscious, that we move and think and talk? I often wonder how it is that anything exists at all. Why is there *something* instead of *nothing*? Over the human centuries, people have had many answers to this question. You might have your own. But the main thing is that the necessary rain falls through air necessary for our lives, is absorbed by the necessary earth that provides our necessary food.

So far as we know, the state of being we call "life" exists only here on this planet. We haven't discovered firm evidence of even one bacteria or cactus or mouse even 60 billion miles away on far stars. Life seems strong on earth, but it is also fragile. Human beings have multiplied—5 billion of us now, and there will probably be 10 billion by the time you Wingate students are 50 years old—but life can disappear in a hurry.

Scientists have tried to spark life in test tubes of various liquids and in chambers filled with gasses, but can't. It seems to be God's secret. I have a hunch it always will be. We can nurture life by treating the earth and ourselves with respect, but we can't create life itself.

Mr. Ehrlich has always been one of those people amazed by everything around him. He's with you to be your teacher and friend, and you're with him to be his teachers and friends, as you hear the world's music—sunshine and rain, voices, objects, dreams. You don't know me, but I'm with you, too, and you're with me in my thoughts, and with me as I write poems.

As I said, you don't know me, but I'm not any kind of special or fancy person. I'm the first in my family who went to college. At 54, I still play basketball, though my knees are sometimes a problem. I like to play poker. I like to read and write. I've been married for 32 years now, and my wife and I have two children. I'm lucky enough to make a living doing something I enjoy, and I wish the same for you. I've learned that if we don't have health and love, we don't have much, if anything. All in all, I'm sort of a shy person, introverted, introspective.

Reading my book *Pterodactyl Rose* with you, Mr. Ehrlich is taking a chance on you. I don't think it's an easy book to read. Poetry is very concentrated, and you have to listen hard, but if you say the words, and if you can get the rhythm, you'll get a feeling for what's going on. This might sound ridiculous to you, but when a poet reads even one of his or her own poems, he or she is also listening hard to what is going on in the secret heart of the poem. The poem is a living thing, just as you are, and can't be pinned down too definitely with definitions. But you can pretty much hear, in general, what a poem is about, how it angles in on the world, and then, by reading again and again, maybe even looking up some words in your dictionary, you can get closer and closer to it until it becomes a friend that's trying to let you in on something complex, something almost beyond words and ideas. (I guess that there are many meanings beyond words that words can suggest.) A poem isn't an editorial in a newspaper. We don't "understand" it the way we understand a math problem. Very often if we describe what a poem is doing, how it works, how it is put together, and what it sounds like, we'll move toward its meanings.

I was born in Brooklyn in 1940 and raised further out on Long Island. I think it was a jolt to my young self suddenly to be out in the country. I've many memories of Hollis and Jamaica, too, and then of Hauppauge and Nesconset, two small towns in Suffolk County. I remember spending much time at ponds and in the woods. I think I realized some things then that I always want to remember. Some of these things are in *Pterodactyl Rose*.

A poem hopes to be a *microcosm*, a small world that has the nature of the whole world. That is, if you read a hard poem like "A Jar" which is about what is called "development" and about what seems to be the threat to an "indicator species," it might come to be for you about construction in your own neighborhood, about a vacant lot you've had your eye on, about someone you know who is like the one worker at the end of the poem who kneels to fill a jar with water and tadpoles. Why does that person do what he does? Maybe he doesn't even know why he does it. And listen to how the speaker, the one telling the story, interprets the events. This poem is a mouthful, I think, as it jams words together as the world gets smaller and smaller for its polliwogs. But if you'll read this poem many times, and get into touch with the speaker, you might hear things that are also in your own heart. Listen to that fourth stanza, the little Eden there that soon disappears.

A Jar

Each noon, at the construction site around the corner
from my own wooded suburban acre,
I checked progress: the bigger trees—almost all ash,
a few maple, one white oak—chainsawed, dragged out
by dozer and chain; then dozer back in for clearing brush;

then dozer, backhoe, and ten-ton roller to cut
foundation-, drainage-, and sewer-pipe patterns
into subsoil and clay, to pack dirt so it would never shift.
Day by day, in drizzle or shower, hot sun
or one sudden out-of-season jet stream shift to chill,

the men widened the site's geometric margins
to where, in one corner, piles of trucked-in sand
diminished a twenty-foot puddle filled for weeks
with thousands of tadpoles just beginning
to grow legs and lose their tails. The time would come,

of course, to fill this last swale. Meanwhile,
the polliwog population prospered in this luke-warm
algae-sweetened pond of their world. . . .
And then was gone, all at once, their birthplace levelled
with sand and a few inches of good topsoil

over which we walked. That was that, except
for this, the one thing, the thing in itself:
how, at about this time, our species began to document
amphibians' disappearance across the globe;
how marshes and swamps were growing silent;

and how, an actor in our sentimental elegy, one worker
placed in his tool chest to take home at quitting time
a jar filled with muddy water and a host of tadpoles,
little blips of sperm-shaped black light.
To catch them, he must have knelt and cupped them in his palms.

I think that my whole book is worried that we are losing our water, our air, our farmland, that we are poisoning ourselves. We seem always very busy thinking about everything except the central problem that we'll eventually have to face. Why do you think it is that we are endangering the ecosystem that supports us? Maybe the poems will be clues. Maybe they will point to the central psychological reasons that we seem to be in trouble.

Read slowly. You can hear the music of a poem by slowing down, listening to how the sounds echo one another. The meanings are in the sounds. Try to keep connecting the poems, feeling how they fit together.

What you're doing is listening closely to another human being talking to you. A poem hopes to be part of a community with you.

Pterodactyl Rose (man, that title just came to me and I got a kick out of it and decided to keep it, I mean the way it joins a fearsome extinct flying reptile with a beautiful flower that we can still experience) may finally be about the one central thing we have to know if we and our children are going to continue living on this planet where the rain still rains for us and the sun still shines. But how would you express what it is we have to know and feel in order to live lives that bless and are blessed? Maybe you'll be writing some of your own poems and "open letters" like this one. When you do, remember the rain and the look in the eyes of someone you love. Remember *specific* things, and these things will come to be about the larger things.

I hope you come to care for a few of these poems. Make believe they're whispering to you about the things that your dreams are trying to tell you. And don't think that the poems are brain-twisters or puzzles. They're songs sung by someone who is yearning for you to understand what he himself is trying to understand. What do you think this is?

I wish I had more time right now to say more things to you. Maybe we'll meet one of these seasons. You take care of yourselves.

I remember Mr. Ehrlich when he was only about 20 years old. Somehow, even then when he was finding himself, he knew he'd someday be with you to help you find your way. I like thinking of this. As you hear this letter of mine, I'll be about 300 miles away, but near. Thanks for listening to some of my poems. To catch them, you might have to kneel and cup them in your palms.

Silver Maple

Does a tree—say that silver maple outside my window—have consciousness? In David Watson's *Beyond Bookchin* (1996), social ecologist Murray Bookchin answers Watson's question as follows: "Give me a chainsaw, and I'll teach you something about consciousness and communication. I'll resolve this discussion fast."

But if I were to take a chainsaw to Bookchin himself, and end his life, would this murder prove that he was never conscious to begin with? His illustration, so cut and dried to him, answers only by way of power, ignorance, violence, and fossil fuel.

However inane Bookchin's retort and certitude, let's simply say that many would agree that trees are not conscious, are not aware of their own existence, thoughts, surroundings, do not appraise their own situations, do not experience joy or pain. And what are the trees missing? Many reasonable people seem to assume that without language, language spoken silently to ourselves or spoken aloud or written to others, we are essentially otherwise and elsewhere, *a*conscious, *non*conscious, *un*conscious and spiritually deprived, maybe alive but vacant of soul at best. I'm not sure where orangutans, parrots and guppies fit into Bookchin's realm of the conscious or unconscious, but surely the stakes here are the highest: to declare that trees have no consciousness is to divide them from ourselves and to make them expendable; to suggest easy and rightful dominion over other existences not aware or awake enough to suffer from what we call shame or degradation, existences that are of no account should their presence come to seem extraneous to us, to our respiration, our sustenance, our communal life, our desire for beauty. (As President Reagan once said, if you've seen one redwood, you've seen them all.) To declare that trees have no consciousness is to reduce them to commodities and to challenge their very right-in-themselves to exist.

Out there in front of me is the growing, leaf-bearing, nest-supporting, rooted and branched entity that I call a silver maple. So far as I know, nothing akin to human language trembles its phloem or xylem. It has no opinion of the seasons, of people, of dogs, of crows or squirrels. Should a hawk devour a mourning dove in its limbs, it will not pray or complain or praise. It just goes on being itself. This is its old story that we've heard since we first named this creature and in so doing separated ourselves from it.

But how to express its non-narrative story? The word "consciousness" won't do. The silver maple's being eludes our abilities to apprehend it. We might be able to take its "pulse," to listen to it as it "listens," to note our observations and then to describe its skills and adaptations as it maintains the life in itself, but we cannot imagine that wordless condition of its ongoingness unless we subside or ascend into its meditative state. I'm reminded of Walt Whitman in "Song of the Open Road": "Why are there trees I never walk under but large and melodious thoughts descend upon me? / (I think they hang there winter and summer on those trees and always drop fruit as I pass)." Under the silver maple, I have had these large and melodious wordless thoughts. Some kind of interchange, I've felt, has taken place—living things aware of one another in fact if not in language. Is this too-too, this declaration of communion, this avowal of what smacks of the shamanism so despised by ultra-rationalists in their square hats? Watson argues for what may be the only balance that can save us: "An evolved reason will have a place for the wolf, for the consciousness of the redwood, for ghost dancers, mystics and animistic tribal villagers—will coax into being, with a little luck, a rounded, vital synthesis of primal, archaic and modern."

We will stand beneath the silver maple and look up into it or close our eyes wherever we are to see it. We will keep saying its name to ourselves until its delimiting name—*silver maple silver maple silver maple silver maple silver maple silver maple silver maple silver maple*—is only a hypnotic trochaic rhythm of sound. . . . And when, after a long time, we come back, we will know we have been there, reverentially, where that Other, that other living thing and we are of the same source and of the same dust and hum. Or else.

Trance

I was sipping coffee, & watercoloring, occasionally dipping my brush into a jelly jar of water to free it before returning to another color or going on to a new one altogether. . . .

Burnt umber, Indian red, ochre, canyon yellow. Even after I'd swallowed the water, I didn't notice until I put the jelly jar down, for my painting had begun to form itself beyond intention. . . .

I washed down the mixture of colors with coffee, & kept painting, as along a valley where buffalo grazed on flowers thousands of years before in my remembering.

Milk Rain

Heavy rain on the prairie, now falling straight down.
The herd keeps feeding, calves keep thrusting
up into their mothers for milk, rain keeps raining

& dripping from the mothers' fur down to udders
into the faces of the feeding calves, rain
mixing with milk on the tongues of the feeding calves.

Tongues

Buffalo tongues were pickled in salt, freightcars of them, & shipped east in a rhythmic industrial music of the mind, millions of tongues passing over our horizontal sleepers, clackety-clack.

I don't know whether they were packed in wooden crates or barrels, or if merchants supplied the hunters & shippers with stoneware vats, the 20 & 50 & 100 galloners that still show up at country auctions. It must have been very dark & very silent inside a vat of tongues.

But I'm wondering, to begin with, how hard it was to cut the tongue out. How rigid were the jaws of the dead animal? Could a right-handed hunter hold down the lower jaw with his right knee while inserting the fingers of his left hand in the nostrils & pulling open the jaws? In this way his right hand would be free to work a knife. But he'd need two hands to cut out the wet tongue, wouldn't he? Maybe it had to be a two-man operation.

They did not have to break out teeth to get to that organ, I'd guess, but how far back did they make their cut? Did they try to get as much root as possible, maybe a little palate, & was the root a darker or fattier meat that chefs were glad to receive?

It must have been arm-wearying work to collect hundreds, thousands, hundreds of thousands of tongues. Were they thrown into salt or a brine solution right away, or put in leather or canvas bags, or Indian baskets, or were they thrown onto a wagon? How much did one weigh? I've read that in the buffalo killers' camps conditions were such that skinning knives also "did duty at the platter," but just how big & what shape was the tongue-knife? Did much blood run from a tongue when it was cut? What colors was the tongue? Was it brown tending toward pink at the edges? Could you see mauve in it, as you can in the leaf of the broad-leafed milkweed still growing in prairie margins? Was there a white froth on it, & did its colors, later, change much? Could you judge its freshness by its colors?

In essence, tongues were made of the grasses & fresh waters of the plains, but did they have, when fresh, any odor—chewed grass mixed with saliva? dusty fur & urine & cottonwood bark? licorice pumice?

I've read that sheep & cattle eat grass to its roots, but buffalo ate only the tender upper shoots & allowed the plains to hold water against floods & to regenerate the grasses & themselves. Did their tongues, therefore, taste juicier & create in you thoughts of mysterious cyclical benevolence as you chewed?

Some of the buffalo must still have been half-alive when their tongues were cut out, & some must still have had beating hearts afterwards. Was the severance a surgical operation, a deft excision, or was the tongue hacked out? What was its texture? Was it smooth to the eye & touch, or was it surprisingly rough like the surface of coral or a bed of bluet anemones? Could you see the taste buds? Could you see the saliva ducts? Was the tongue bifurcated underneath like a heart? When you tried to pull it out, did attaching muscles cling to it like the chalazae of an egg or the tough strands that fasten a bivalve's body to its shell?

Did the tongue quiver when removed as though it were still trying to lap water? Did it swell quickly, or did it seem to lose bulk in the air? Did any of the hunters eat tongue raw as some people today eat special cuts of beef? Were tongues that should have been passed over ever harvested from decrepit or diseased animals? Were some tongues ulcerated or pocked with sores?

I've read various estimates of the number of buffalo that lived on the plains before the white onslaught. 30-60,000,000. By 1888 maybe a thousand survived. Today, the gene-pool must be dangerously shallow, only a glaze now after those millions of years of thunder & rain.

Crazy Horse Mnemonic

When the heavens thunder, it is the herds, or thunder.
When the herds thunder, it is the heavens, or the herds—
dark brown & black over the sacred land, the color of sound.

When the ground thunders, it is the herds of the heavens.
When the heavens thunder, it is the herds of the ground—
dark brown & black over the sacred land, the color of sound.

The herds thunder across the heavens. The herds
thunder over the ground—dark brown & black, black
& dark brown over the sacred land, the color of sound.

In summer, the killing & cutting must have been work engulfed in
bloodsmell & flies; in winter, clumsy work with gloves pushing through
ice-shagged fur.

We know that a hunter could shoot one animal & the others would
stay with it & with one another until the whole herd was dead except
for the bawling calves that were not worthy of or did not require bullets.
Did the hunters generally let these calves be, or did they cut their
throats & take their tongues as special delicacies?

I'm sure the hunters were not sentimentalists & didn't spend any
time staring into eyes, but were the animals' eyes usually open or closed
when their tongues were taken? When the animals fell, did they
sometimes bite off the tips of their own tongues?

Were the tongues of the bulls different in other ways than weight
from those of the cows? Did the animals groom one another with their
tongues? Did the buffalo sleep standing or lying down, & when they
slept, did the tongue hang from the open mouth, or did it press against
the back of the upper teeth in a moderate vacuum to keep it from
obstructing the passage of air? Was the tongue useful for cutting grass as
the animals browsed, or did it instinctively remain back in the mouth
out of the way of the teeth? Did buffalo snore?

Just how tough was the tongue? Did it thwack through thorns &
blade-sided grasses? Did a chef have to tenderize it with a mallet to break
down its musculature before cooking? Was it a meat that could fry or
broil in its own fats, or did you need lots of butter to keep it from sticking
to iron? Before one of their debates, Abraham Lincoln & Stephen
Douglas feasted on buffalo tongue. Did Edgar Allan, Emily, or Walt ever
taste it?

Did tongue dry well for jerky? Were bits of it sprinkled on salads?
Were tongues stuffed with vegetables & crabmeat?

I've read that in an eastern city you could buy a passenger pigeon
for a penny. How much for a pound of hickory- or oak-smoked tongue,
which had to come from further away? In the cities, was buffalo tongue

a curiosity, something like alligator or bear or beefalo meat today, or did it become for a decade or two standard fare, even a staple? I can almost hear the butcher saying, "Here ya are, Mrs. Newlyn, a beautiful cut," can almost hear the merchants & houseboys & cooks slapping the heavy slabs of tongue onto wood counters & into drysinks.

Do you know the Georgia O'Keeffe painting of a steerskull twined with roses afloat in blue sky over a barren landscape? In place of that skull I see in my mind's eye a flayed-out buffalo tongue.

Long slices of tongue were sometimes dipped in batter & fried, or grilled, or baked, & chunks were stirred into stews, & there were choice steaks ordered rare or medium or well-done & served with dark American beers & French wines. Diners at first must have pictured the animals as they ate, but then the meat must have become the usual blur of habit.

Did your own tongue, when it contacted & manipulated that other tongue in your mouth . . . I can't seem to frame the question.

What was a tongue's consistency when you chewed? Did flavor & consistency depend on the time of year the buffalo were killed & the lushness of the plains' seasonal grasses, or did the buffalo, exept in winter, always manage to keep pace with the ramifying growth? Did a winter tongue possess a winter tang?

Was there a difference between the taste of the tongues of buffalo Indian-run off ravines & free-fallen in dream-panicky air, & buffalo shot business-like & dropped instantaneously dead from a distance? Does fear become taste?

Suppose a big kill, the tongues removed, the hunters gone back to camp or saloon. Full moon above the thousand carcasses where they fell. Wolves that had heard gunfire & come from twenty miles around & waited for dusk when the dead herd would be left to them. Did the wolves eat the humps or flesh sides & ribs first, or go for the viscera, & maybe the liver? Maybe the buffaloes' lips. Living snout to dead snout. Living wolf cubs playing & learning among the dead buffalo. In summer, how many days of eating before the meat was too rancid & maggot-ridden for the wolves, eagles, crows, rats?

Was tongue, prepared as a delicacy with rose petals & cream, an aphrodisiac? . . . One night after killing buffalo with Grand Duke Alexis of Russia, one of our iron heroes slept under the stars:

Tongue

A buffalo cow drank from a tub
in which Custer was dreaming a bath.
She didn't see him under the water,
must be. He watched her tongue
slip in & out of the waterline,
in & out. She left. He lifted up,
breaking staves with his erection. . . .

In that other life of ours we might, in 1850 say, have bought a steak
at our butcher's, taken it home, unwrapped it from the waxed paper
moist with reddish salt, & cut thin pieces from it to fry in our skillet with
butter & leeks, our own tongues watering for the wild buffalo of the
plains that would soon enter our bloodstreams in Philly or New York.

Cereal Craft

For years now, getting away from carcinogenic and cholesterolic bacon and eggs, I've been having cereal for breakfast. I like to slice a banana into my cereal, too.

For a couple of years I'd peel the banana and slice. I like thin slices best, but sometimes hunks of the banana would come off (especially during the fast-ripening summer months) and I'd later have to slice these hunks with my spoon in the cereal. A spoon, of course, is not handy for slicing, but I like a little bit of banana with each spoonful of cereal, so I'd try to slice the awkward assymetrical hunks with my spoon.

One day, before adding banana into my cereal—I'm not sure what made me do this—I sliced the whole banana in half, lengthwise, first. Then, of course, when I sliced the banana into my cereal, I had pieces half the size of my vertical slices! A few days later, I sliced the whole banana in half lengthwise, and then lengthwise again, at right-angle, of course, to my first cut. Then, when I sliced the banana into my cereal, I ended up with symmetrical wedges one fourth the size of each verticle cut. And I've tried even more lengthwise cuts, and other fancy variations of cuts—angles and wavery lines—but have found that the banana does best with just the two initial lengthwise cuts before the verticle slicing. You can go too far and turn the banana into a mush fit only for banana bread. I'm glad I tried more and various cuts, though, or I'd always have been curious about other possible effects.

Often when I sliced the banana, the peel I had peeled away got in the way. I couldn't take the whole peel off and then slice, of course, because it got too messy, so I tried to hold on to the peel, which got in the way of my knife, and it's awkward to peel part of the banana, and then a couple inches more and then a couple inches more. Then, one day, accidentally or intuitively, I tore two pieces of peel all the way off from only the top of the banana, keeping just the bottom of the peel, and this worked like a charm. I had enough peel to grip without getting bananary fingers, and there was a bonus: the bottom peel kept me from cutting my fingers when I sliced through the banana. I've gotten to be adept at handling the banana in this way, and I've been happy, lately, with this whole methodology.

Usually, when my bits of banana dropped into my cereal, a few rolled oats or wheatflakes or a raisin would jump out of the bowl. I had to pick such detritus off the counter or floor. I hated to decide, too, so early in the morning, whether to put these errant bits of cereal into the garbage or back into my bowl. It was too early in the day to deal with questions of science and health (germs) or ethics (starving people). (One morning, kneeling on the floor as though in prayer, I even found myself worrying that maybe a Third World tarantula had made its way to my kitchen along with my bunch of bananas and, gentle a creature as it was reputed to be, had had about enough of American life and was aching to inject venom into the fat white American hand reaching toward it under the table.) As an ugly American, I give to charities as I need to think well of myself, and just wished that my morning cereal had stayed in its bowl to begin with.

But then one day, without thinking, I simply sliced my banana into my bowl first! When I poured the cereal onto the sliced banana, the cereal stuck to it, didn't jump at all. Wonderful. And this way I didn't have to keep spooning and stirring some slices of banana to the bottom of the cereal. Banana comes up naturally, now, as I eat the cereal, spoonful by spoonful.

Over the years, I've made even further improvements. As I said, you can go too far, but I guess I'll be okay if, above all, I keep concentrating on the banana's taste which is now interfused with the pleasure it has been and will continue to be to find ways to get my bowl of cereal ready in the first place.

New Moon

Archibald MacLeish once wrote me that he'd been reading Robert Fitzgerald's *Odyssey*—reading aloud to his wife "under the hum of the reef off the south shore of Bermuda"—had gotten to the moment in Book Eleven when Alkinoös, King of the Phaiákians, says to Odysseus, "you told as a poet would, a man who knows the world. . . ." "That last line," wrote MacLeish, "was like the bursting of a sun. . . . What else is a great poet! A man who knows the world. Who else knows the world? Who else but Shakespeare, Dante, Homer himself. . . . magnificent phrase . . . I now have the word for it—a man who knows the world."

Driving home late last night along a country road I looked up at the moon and confirmed for myself for the first time an image in "Sir Patrick Spens" I'd never quite appreciated before: "Late, late yestre'en I saw the new moon / Wi' the auld moon in hir arm. . . ." A crescent of new moon seemed to be holding what was left of the old moon's gray head within her golden curve. Did I feel vaguely uncomfortable, perhaps connecting with some human dread of the old in process of being consumed by the new?: "And I fear, I fear, my dear master, / That we will come to harm." I don't know. I know too much about the moon now, maybe, to feel the foreboding I'd have felt centuries ago seeing the phase I saw. I've seen a man step down onto the moon. I've seen moon rocks. But late last night I saw the body's curve of the ancient new moon as she held her own past self. I am now a better reader of the awful old ballad whose author or authors knew the world I seem to be losing.

The Other

We are spellbound with things inside of things—bits of root and feather and bone and dried skin in medicine bags, postage stamps in albums in slipcases, gemstone scarabs in the mouths of mummies in coffins, silver goblets in sacristies, gold coins in pouches in safes in the hulls of sunken ships, hidden chambers in pyramids, the contents of oak trunks in secret rooms in castles—whatever holds to its own power, and then releases that power as we expose or unfold it with hands, heart, mind, then concentrates its power again as we replace its cover, close its cabinet, click its lid shut, return it to a darkness that over the course of time will always again intensify its mystery.

Nature, too, enclosing itself, creation within creation: eggs in hexagonal cells, the innermost queen in her chamber beneath the ground or within the tree, flesh bodies in shells, seeds in spine-covered pods, the inner ear and inner eye, the double-helix of genes in which we reside in our ancient future, brains in skulls, sperm cells in sacs, the unborn whale or human child floating in its warm womb within its ocean of water or air, ferns preserved in the stomachs of mammoths in glacial ice, our life-bearing earth within its galactic system of consciousness and time.

Words, too: that which waits within a sounded rhythm, the pale flare of image or place that needs the oxygen and acetylene torch of intelligence or conflagration of memory to awaken us again, the poem with its line-corridors closed on walls behind which libraries await discovery, or which spiral downward into stairways with landings where the world's goods—a phial containing one of Jesus's tears or drops of blood, a luna moth in its cocoon, a Civil War bullet buried in a beech branch—come to meaning as our spirits ascend to that hiddenness beyond matter.

This is the other that we intimate we are. Everything inside of everything—to be seen and heard and almost understood. To be known, then left to ourselves again to wait inside ourselves until the next revelation.

The Idea

After her mastectomy, my wife began reconstruction. It was what she wanted—her clothes would fit better, her posture would remain balanced.

Across the equator of what had been her breast, through where her nipple had been, her scar was like a smile, an ascending lifeline crosscut by dozens of stitches. I didn't understand the intricacies of reconstruction, but a rubber breast-shaped container was eventually inserted, and a quarter-cup of saline solution was injected into the swelling container every couple of weeks, the skin stretching rosily around it. It was during this time that I got my idea.

I wondered if the surgeon could create a pocket inside my wife's new breast. My wife and I could keep C-notes in that pocket where, surely, they'd be safe. We could keep some rare gold coins there in case inflation or war hit this country so hard that we'd need gold to swap for bread and eggs or to buy our lives from invading hordes. We could keep an extra set of car keys in that pocket in her breast. Maybe our children could fit inside that pocket, and maybe theirs, maybe our house, my study and books and all my poems, maybe a bomb shelter where I could rest and be able to hear her heartbeat, always.

Ellipsis

The physical world is evidence, yes, but of what?. . .

We can locate only one constant in poetry: desire, the desired world. Rhythm, image, coherence, etc.—just symptoms, just indications of this desire. . . .

A poem's truths have little to do with the truths of science (blah, blah), *that* particular grounding, *that* "reality.". . . A poem's burden is to convince us of its truth while we are sounding it, to become our breath and belief until its last syllable diminishes beyond at least conscious attention, as it must—Frost's "momentary stay against confusion," Stevens's "supreme fiction" (our belief in something we know is not true) in miniature operation in each poem. The poet Thomas McGrath says, "I'd rather listen to what a really gifted bullshit artist can do any day than listen to some undertaker's report." This speaks to the fact that our real world materially and factually apprehended now in its increasing toxicity would read like a post-mortem, yes, but McGrath's emphasis is on the desire, the "I'd rather . . . any day.". . .

Whatever their surface subjects or methods—even poems that seem to be primarily about their minds as they engage language unfolding into the present— contemporary poems, defending themselves and us from this brave new world, sometimes with the indeterminicies of John Ashbery's most characteristic poems and sometimes with the declarations of Allen Ginsberg's and sometimes elsewise, become more and more poignant in this yearning, this desire. . . .

At the Gate

In *The Government of the Tongue* (1988) Seamus Heaney tells us that in 1972 he was on his way with a friend to a Belfast recording studio to make a tape of songs and poems when "explosions occurred in the city and the air was full of the sirens of ambulances and fire engines." The two friends cancelled their plans: "The very notion of beginning to sing at that moment when others were beginning to suffer seemed like an offense against their suffering."

"Seemed like" is the fulcrum phrase. Heaney, understandably, is determined to affirm the act and art of poetry, no matter what. He says that he came to feel that he and his friend were mistaken not to have made their tape. "Did we not see that song and poetry added to the volume of good in the world?" *The Government of the Tongue* becomes a defense of poetry in the great tradition of such defenses. We witness Heaney's very human need to go on writing despite fears that have been with him from the beginning. The essence of these fears is revealed in an ominous dream he recounts in *Preoccupations* (1980), his first book of essays: "I was shaving . . . when I glimpsed in the mirror a wounded man falling towards me with his bloodied hands lifted to tear at me or to implore." Now, writing the new essays of *Government*, Heaney says, helped him *allay* the fear that "in arrogating to oneself the right to take refuge in form, one is somehow denying the claims of the beggar at the gate."

From all that I've seen, read, realized since my rural Long Island boyhood, I've come to believe that over the next 75–150 years we will draw close to the as yet unimagined end of our existence on this planet. We are fouling our habitat beyond redemption. Quickly and surely we are dying out. The evidence is all around us and within us, and is obvious to those of us who can at least now and then shake ourselves out of the trance of habit and ongoingness that is our usual life.

Though in the end, of course, the two spheres are not divisible, Heaney's struggle to believe that poetry is viable and necessary takes place, as does Anna Akhmatova's, Czeslaw Milosz's, or Wole Soyinka's, against a political, not ecological background. And it may be (or it may not be) that until all people are free, in Northern Ireland or in the Soviet Union or in Eastern Europe or in Africa or in the United States, we will not be able to come together as human beings to realize and do something about—if this is at all still possible, and this becomes increasingly doubtful—what we are doing to sweep ourselves under history's rug. The two spheres are not divisible, finally, but I want *directly* to raise Heaney's stakes here: If we continue as we are now, it does not look as though the human species will survive for even two more centuries, or will survive only in radically impoverished remnants. Given this, should anyone continue spending time writing poetry? Should not each of us, instead, devote our efforts every possible minute personally and communally to eliminating carcinogens from the food chain, to cleaning our air and water, to preserving undeveloped green space? Wouldn't it make more sense to spend our time, instead of making poems and books of poems, lobbying politicians (who in general do not and will not, nor will their constituents, read poetry) toward life-sustaining priorities?

During centuries when we've seemed to have all of Time for questions of aesthetics, we have asked in a hundred ways whether poetry could make anything happen. Now, we approach a time when we will not be able to breathe, when rising temperature and ocean levels and systemic poisons will wipe us out. Now, the answer matters. Can a poem stop even one suburbanite in this democracy from spraying toxic chemicals on his or her lawn because of some idiot's notion of what a weed is? Will a poem convince us to plant trees and to reject rain forest hamburger lunches? What *is* it, exactly, that can save us, if anything can, and can poetry be any part of this salvation? As we stare at it, as we sound it, as we filter it from ourselves, can it help us to change our lives?

Almost everything we now hear about poetry assumes that the poem need only be true while we are inside it, that it creates its own cosmos, that the poet's task is to convince us of the poem's assumptions while we are in its presence, and that, later, the world must of course arrive with its challenges, its "buts," until the next reading restores the poem's world again. What's not to love about this fluid sense of the poem? In Robert Frost's famous phrase, poetry is a "momentary stay against confusion," and Heaney echoes this here when he says that "when the lyric discovers its buoyant completion . . . a plane is—

fleetingly—established where the poet is intensified in his being and freed from his predicaments." "Fleetingly"—Heaney interrupts himself to make sure of this qualification and diminishment. William Stafford has said that in a poem he wants to feel free to go in any direction. (There is a loving trust of human nature in this, the opposite of Thoreau's absolutist couplet "Man is the Devil / The source of all evil.") Well, in our time poets feel free to go in any direction—in fact, we have evolved a rarefied aesthetics that banishes poetry of strong and abiding conviction from the castle—but our direction as a species now is into absolute death and we may well wonder if there should be any more so-called poetry at all, all that artistic and self-satisfied stuff in poets' books and in anthologies, all that clever and sometimes moving and almost always useless stuff we hear at readings because poets have been "arrogating to [themselves] the right to take refuge in form" while plants and animals find no refuge from us and die out.

The earth is dying, but how can I stop reading writers I admire, for example, and how can I stop writing when, after so many years of absorption in the process, the writing seems to be writing me, seems to be what I have come to be? If I'm wasting my energies, given these stakes, on something trivial and indulgent, I want to know.

As a divided person, as someone on the edge of insanity whenever I truly imagine, as I do for only a second or three once in a while, what is becoming of us, I want to argue two things at once. One, that even a poem ostensibly about, say, someone who stops with his horse by woods on a snowy evening and comes to consider his death, or about the desire to sail to a Byzantium out-of-nature where artificial birds sing of three dimensions of time, even poems "about" subjects seemingly unrelated to the diseased ecosystem of the earth, are at the same time always "about" something else, the *central* something. All fully-realized poetry has to do with our common humanity as we look around and within us to discover, by intuition and austere thought, by leaps of imagination and by logic, what we are. All fully-realized poetry, whatever its surface subject or story, is about the mystery of and possibility of human community. We are born, aspire, love, have children, experience joy and suffering, and we die, together. All fully-realized poetry in whatever form, rendered by whatever associational and/or narrative and/or imagistic and/or abstract and/or surrealistic and/or objective means, is at root about what we are together, what we have in common. And it may be that such realizations which, in the end, point up the absurdity and foolishness of greed and of personal and national selfishness, are our only hope.

But I want to argue at the same time that contemporary poetry, given what is happening to us now—there are no precedents—given the obvious possibility/probability of near extinction before even two more centuries of poetry can be winnowed for the anthologies of the non-human future, contemporary poetry no longer suffices. Now, surely, it is not direct enough. It is too slippery, too reticent, too satisfied, too elitist, too modulated, too slant. Its first rules are subtlety, suggestion, and subtext. It does not establish values. It plays. It is the packaged product of an age of situational ethics. And it is unread except by those of us who make it and who share, without realizing it or without caring, an ethereal and specialized language. For the first time in our history it is a matter of life or death to us that our arts mean and matter. Unless the poetry we are now writing changes, it should desist. It should run off with its tail between its legs. Now, as the dark gets darker, as the topsoil of our American Midwest, only half as deep as it was in the mid 1800's, continues to diminish and the Great Mall grows inside us, our poetry is, in the main, only a sophisticated plaything. We "educated" elitists who have supported it and written it need to change our lives with our poetry, or need to shut up and instead work in practical ways on our own or with others within the imaginative organizations trying to drag their feet against the oblivion into which we are falling.

We are dying out, and dying out fast. The world's population will triple over the next century—one person a second being added to the population of India, e.g., about seventeen million a year, until India will surely become, alternately, a mud bog and a dust howl (I'll let the typo stand)—and then, it appears, we will be gone. Meanwhile, the next poem you read in *The New Yorker* or in *American Poetry Review* or in a poet's book, the next poem you hear during a PBS special, whatever its ostensible subject, may ultimately be (probably, because of its unconscious symbolic sourses, cannot help being) about our common humanity, Walt Whitman's "common air that bathes the globe," but who will know this except the specialist? Poetry itself is one of the distractions keeping us from dealing with that fast-approaching time when no one will be alive to turn the pages of a book or to tune in a poetry program from the BBC. You and I, as specialists, have not, for one reason or another, spoken straight-out or acted on the truths we know and feel. Or we've suffered from a lack of imagination that has kept us from realizing that all poetry is about to go blank. Or we have been inept in finding ways by which poetry can effect change.

The concept Heaney keeps coming back to in *The Government of the Tongue* is "efficacy." During the act of poetry, he says, the tongue becomes ungoverned. When it does, "It gains access to a condition that is unconstrained and, while not being practically effective, is not necessarily inefficatious." But to be a philosopher, Thoreau says, is to solve some of the practical problems of life, and I need to eliminate in myself what I now believe to be rationalizations when I begin to consider things merely "not . . . practically effective [but] not necessarily inefficacious." Our poetry continues dreaming contentedly along (it does not know that it is dreaming) inside this aesthetic of inefficacy while we lose the world. Heaney speaks of poetry as possessing "its own vindicative force," its own "dispensation." He quotes Polish poet Anna Swir who says that the poet, during the writing of the poem, "for one moment . . . possesses wealth usually inaccessible to him, and he loses it when that moment is over." "For one moment"—here's that butterfly-like concept of poetry again while species of real butterflies disappear forever. Heaney concludes that "Poetry's special status among the literary arts derives from the audience's readiness to concede to it a similar efficacy and resource." Just what audience is that, if not an audience of the passive, or dreamers who spend their time loving the poem for its own sake while nature, the progenitor and source of all poetry, withers? And just what "efficacy" is that? Poetry has not been, to call up the dictionary definition of efficacious, "effective as a means, measure, remedy." Nor, given its current course, given Heaney's representative yearning for the old way, the old rationalizations, however eloquently this splendid poet speaks them, can it possibly be. To justify my own life in poetry, I want badly to believe what Heaney says, but nothing seems to be slowing, much less reversing, our acceleration toward death, and I have come to feel that if poetry cannot be efficacious in direct and practical ways, then it should retire to its

126

laboratory or parsonage or library or parlor or art gallery and moulder until the end, until the last visitor knocking on its gate staggers away in poisonous body to gasp his or her last poisonous breath.

Rounding toward conclusion of his title essay Heaney says, "Here is the great paradox of poetry and the imaginative arts in general." Faced with the brutality of the historical onslaught, they are "practically useless . . . In one sense the efficacy of poetry is nil—no lyric has ever stopped a tank. It is like the writing in the sand in the face of which accusers and accused are left speechless and renewed." He quotes John's Gospel in which the Pharisees tempt Jesus to condemn an adulteress. Should she be stoned? they ask. "But Jesus stooped down, and with his finger wrote in the ground, as though he heard them not." Poetry is like Jesus' writing, Heaney says. "It does not propose to be instrumental or effective. Instead in the rift between what is going to happen and whatever we should wish to happen, poetry holds attention for a space, functions not as distraction but as pure concentration, a focus where our power to concentrate is concentrated back on ourselves." Yes, Heaney is surely right. This is what poetry has been for us, but it has not been enough. It has not searched hard enough to forge the weapons of imagination and the word that can help in the immediate battle for our existence even a half-dozen generations from now. We have not let poetry "propose to be instrumental or effective." Let us now do so. Poetry, if this is possible—and if it is not then we need to sacrifice, need to abandon it, need to desist from its pleasures and instead become practically effective in other ways—must do more than "hold attention for a space."

In an essay on media censorship of the essential news of our time, Daniela Gioseffi asks, "Are you guilty, guilty, guilty all the time because you know the radical truth and don't even have time to read it, let alone contribute to it after you've subscribed to it? Rest assured, dear nearly extinct reader, that you're not alone!" Surely poets now know "the radical truth," but we are in the main, as Gioseffi implies, sick at heart and confused. We have not yet committed ourselves to embodying it in our work, and we feel guilty. Once we do, we will find the means. Or, if we can't . . .

Polish labor leader and politician Lech Walesa said in November of 1989 to a joint session of Congress, "We have heard many beautiful words of encouragement . . . but, being a worker and a man of concrete work, I must tell you that the supply of words on the world market is plentiful, but the demand is falling." Poetry has become plentiful and cheap. It has disavowed the possibility that it has concrete work to do, and might be able to do it. If poetry cannot realize that all humanity is at the gate, if something necessarily fleeting and inefficacious dwells in its heart, if it cannot face the probability of its own extinction and must claim dispensation, must endlessly lose itself within the subtleties of its own processes, if it is only for our leisure hours when life seems good to us, abiding, worthwhile, let us find this out, too, so that we can stop deluding ourselves. Let us be poets enough to see and embody and act upon what Jesus wrote in the earth. When the radical evidence around us is lit with shafts of intuition, we do know, don't we? If we don't reject Heaney's "Poetry is more a threshold than a path," we are, finally, doomed. We must become the path. Let us as poets try now as never before to reach the bottom of the sludge of our evasions, to cut through the rotten aesthetics of our tradition. Let us write poems we can carry in our pockets and will listen to each time we spend our money. Let us try, directly, practically, by way of our poetry, to save the world for future generations of our children, or let us shut up and get to work in other ways. Jesus wrote in the dirt what the Pharisees in their hearts had been given to know: that the woman was to be loved, not stoned.

Sacred Groves

Some wooded slopes are too steep to plow and plant, but contemporary poetry has been thundering up into them with its machines, clearing & grading & planting, getting one or two crops at most. The abused slopes will no longer hold the rain, are gullying and blowing away, ruined, no longer useful for human beings as intermediary between their daily selves of bread and their souls. It will be many years, if ever, before this land supports even weeds and field mice again. . . .

The New American Poetry

It is the poetry of the privileged class.

It inherits portfolios.

It was born in the Ivy League, and inbred there.

Its parents filled its homes with bubbling Bach,
    silver and crystal brightnesses for its surfaces
    which do not sweat to wring meaning from paychecks.

It does not hear the cheap and natural music of the cow.

Its vases hold platinum-stemmed roses, not ponds with logs
    from which turtles descend at our approach, neckfold
    leeches shining like black droplets of blood.

It swallows Paris and Athens, tracks its genes to the Armory Show.

As it waits by their coffins in the parlor, it applies rouge to Poe and
    Beau Brummell.

Its father is Gertrude Stein, not Whitman, who despises it,
    though it will not admit it.

Old women with children do not live in it.

It does not harvest thought or associate with farmers.

It does not serve in the army, or follow a story.

It revels in skewed cubes, elliptical appositions.

It is inviolate, buttressed by its own skyhook aesthetics.

Ultramarine critics praise it, wash their hands of subject matter.

It is tar-baby without the baby, without the tar.

Its city is not the city of pavement or taxis, business or bums.

It dwells on absence and illusion, mirrors refulgent flames.

Deer that browse beneath its branches starve.

Its emotions do not arise from sensible objects.

It passes rocks as though they were clouds.

It sustains itself on paperweight petals.

It does not flood out its muskrats.

It does not define, catalog, testify, or witness.

It holds models before the young of a skillful evasion, withering
    heartlessness.

It lifts its own weight for exercise, does not body-block,
    or break up double plays, or countenance scar tissue.

It flails in the foam, but has no body and cannot drown.

In his afterlife, Rimbaud smuggles it along infected rivers.

(1982)

Elvis on Velvet

What do you love when you love Elvis?

I would have followed him to the end of his coeternal life in me. But, later on, fat, onstage, the dopehead laughed or sneered as he sang even his early songs, in which I lived

From the time of his first movie in 1956, I surfed and raced with him, Hawaii to Indianapolis, but the parabola was downward into depression. O Holyrood! By the time of his death, I was in deep dream analysis. I learned that I had calcified into his twin under his breast-bone.

I bought my first Elvis on Velvet at a service station in 1978. It was pompadour and rhinestone, inky night and rouge. I called it "Synonym in Gauche." A few days later I found another, "Our Silken Leather Puppet of the Sacred Buckle," at a garage sale. Now, I have dozens of him, all in one room. When I feel his Vegas cape against my ear, when his velour heart beats too close to mine, I sit in that room in a barber chair in which he once sat and spin myself around and play the tracks of two or three of those movies at the same time—advanced aversion therapy.

But I'm allowed, still, to love him, so it's all right, mama, that whenever I leave that room I make myself a cup of coffee, put on a Sun sessions album, and, while he sings "Trying to Get to You" or "I Forgot to Remember to Forget" or "Mystery Train," stare at a black and white photograph I took of him at a fair in Tennessee, so long ago, when he was Elvis Presley.

Fame

For the past week, in the presence of Miranda Whipple, Mitter's member had pressed against his underpants and shorts. The two colleagues had worked hard here in the Gobi rocks, had been all business as they bent and dug for dinosaur fossils, but her perfumed perspiration seemed to enter his nostrils as elementally as did the desert dust, and he wasn't entirely sure that she wasn't feeling the same stirrings in her genitalia as he felt in his. Sometimes, on her knees, the top two buttons of her khaki shirt undone, she looked back at him and smiled with what seemed to him both longing and anticipation, as though her next spade of sand might reveal what each had been looking for for his or her whole life, he, Mitter, of Yale, and she, Whipple, of the State University of New York at Binghamton. They'd been looking for a find of such enormous consequence that a reputation might be assured: *Mitteropterous*, he muttered to himself; *Whipplesaurus*, she mused. Who would be first?

They slept apart, on opposite sides of their fire in a cul-de-sac of rocks that seemed to them to brood secrets. If only these rocks could talk, Mitter muttered; if only these rocks could sing, Whipple mused.

On the morning in question they were working close to one another on an eroded slope of particular promise. Mitter, only half aware of what was happening, found himself moving toward her from her left side, and was at length close enough to touch her. Whipple, her right-hand spade dug in, looked over to her left at him, straightened up—he saw the beautiful bulb of her right breast as she did so—pulled strands of hair from her eyes with the ringless fingers of her left hand, and wet her lips with her tongue. He moved to her quickly, his right hip against her left, his hands rounding over her shoulders. She dropped the spade. He moved his hands down her trembling ribs and pulled out her shirt-tails. He laced his fingers over her firm abdomen as she looked up to him, her eyes closed, for what would surely be the kiss that would seal their lives together. Whipple closed her eyes. Feeling disembodied, acting as though by the volition of his member straining against his shorts, Mitter moved his lips in close proximity to hers.

At that instant, past her lovely face, he saw it: Through the eroded cap of what had been a huge egg appeared the fragile fossilized bones of a 100-million-year-old unhatched dinosaur. There could be no mistake. Its ankle bones angled lupward and identified it as a theropod, an upright hunter akin to a velociraptor; its skull, curled toward its knees in a fetal position, was that of an oviraptor, a long-necked predator something like a vicious ostrich with dagger teeth and reptilian tail. Surely, this creature would be positively identified, the first ever found in its embryonic stage, as a meat-eater!

Flashed in Mitter's mind a picture of himself at a podium. Was that the Swedish king seated in front of him? The lights were blinding.

His fingers moved upward to cup Whipple's breasts. His lips hovered a millimeter from hers. Her perspiration and perfume and the desert dust commingled in the nostrils of his groin. Which would it be, the lady or the dinosaur?

Post Mortem: Literary Criticism

When William Butler Yeats was young he was worried that his taste was too eclectic, that he cared for too many different kinds of poetry. I've wondered about this, about whether caring for various poets, as I do, is an indication of large-heartedness or of a lack of taste and discrimination, of character.

But sometimes, on clear and simple days, dogmatic days, I know what I do and don't like, know how to diagnose poems' diseases. On those days I say to myself, "What the hell, it's easy to weigh and measure poems. Stop second-guessing yourself. Keep your eyes open and remember the zennist who collected 'honey' for farmers and could tell a family's illnesses even before symptoms appeared." On such days, judgment is simple:

Post Mortem: Literary Criticism

If the poem's blood is black with a bad odor:
    infection;
if its white muscle-tissue has yellowed: liver
    disfunction;

if its intestines are lurid purple:
    inflammation;
if its stomach shines abnormally red:
    congestion;

if there are pustules and knots on its lungs:
    tuberculosis;
if there are pink spots about its ribs:
    cholera;

if its spleen is enlarged and filled with blackish pulp:
    tick fever;
if its heart valves are broken: old age,
    or over-exertion.

Refrain

Each year at Herb's annual physical his doctor, an old friend, said to him, "Herb, you've got to stop smoking." Herb said, "I know."

Four years ago Herb developed a severe cough. His doctor listened to his chest, staring off into space. He knuckle-thumped Herb's breastbone. He prescribed antibiotics for Herb's bronchitis. "Herb," he said, "you've got to stop smoking." Herb said, "I know."

Last year Herb noticed a tinge of rose in his sputum. His doctor ordered chest x-rays and after viewing them said, "Herb, now you might as well keep smoking."

Titles: The Ruby

Years before, a man had bought an expensive wooden statue of Jesus that was advertised to contain in its chest a gemstone heart. For decades the man, when he looked at Jesus, imagined that precious heart, but during grievous times in his life he was sometimes uncertain it was truly there.

This is the day we will watch him cut the statue into several pieces, then place these into his fireplace and burn them. He will warm his hands by this fire, meaning no disrespect, loving his savior just the same but needing evidence of the holy gemstone heart for which he had paid so dearly those many years before.

The pieces of statue will burn and turn slowly to ash. With warmed hands, the man will poke through the ashes. We will watch him until the ash gives up Jesus's heart, if it will.

Our title seems to hope and believe it will.

Gospel

After his long papacy distinguished by a conservatism that some even called reactionary, our ascetic Holy Father decided to retire. He had always wanted to conduct research, and this desire was now so intense that it reminded him of terrible sexual pressures he had felt during his early manhood. It was as though, now, God were speaking to him, urging him to fulfill himself completely and to reward himself for decades of selfless deprivation by spending his last years in the thrall of research.

Come to his new estate, he inquired where he could find the earliest manuscripts of the Bible. The library to which a group of cardinals directed him existed almost entirely beneath the gardens of the Vatican itself. Day after day for years he decended the hundreds of curving stone steps to where the ancient and long-ignored papyrus and vellum texts had murmured only to one another for centuries.

One day we librarians heard his shout from down below. "There's an 'r,'" he was heard to exclaim. *"There's an 'r.'"* The sound of "r" reached surface as though spoken from a tomb. What did our Holy Father mean? Had he lost his mind in those dank recesses? We were afraid to go to him as, all day long, we heard his repeated declaration, *"There's an 'r.'"*

That midnight, His Holiness rose from his studies. Disheveled, eyes glazed, he could only whisper to what had now become our curious multitude, "There's an 'r.' It's '*celebrate*'."

Poverty

The central dilemma of criticism: To inquire what poetry is/what the true experience of poetry is, we must divide ourselves, part of us paying rational attention, gauging and weighing what the rapt listener, our other self, hears and feels.

Because of the nature of its medium, words (words spoken *in time*, i.e., measured), a poem possesses a dimension of meaning that painting, music, sculpture do not have. This dimension forms in us as we read, as we conceptualize in other words the suggestions for us of these particular words in time. But even as we do so, we divide the poem, separating the effects of its measures in us from the meanings of the words. "Unawareness of one's feet is the mark of a pair of shoes that fits," says Chuang Tse. Unawareness of parts of a poem (or, to put it another way, *full* awareness of all parts simultaneously) is our hope. The rhythm of the words creates, in part, the meanings of those words, and the meanings of those words create rhythms in us by way of our feelings. In poems, rhythm is rhyme and meanings rhyme.

In his essay "The Poet" Emerson quotes "the wise Spenser"—

> So every spirit, as it is most pure,
> And hath in it the more of heavenly light,
> So it the fairer body doth procure
> To habit in, and it more fairly dight,
> With cheerful grace and amiable sight.
> For, of the soul, the body form doth take,
> For soul is form, and doth the body make.

"Here," Emerson says, "we find ourselves, suddenly, not in the pleasant walks of critical speculation, but in a holy place, and should go very warily and reverently. We stand before the secret of the world,—there where Being passes into Appearance, and Unity into Variety."

The true experience of poetry, not computer poetry or experimental poetry or cowboy poetry or avant-garde poetry or language poetry or ethnic poetry or humorous poetry but poetry, is the experience of

Emerson's Unity, the unity of the undivided generative force of the universe, or, in slightly more religious terms, of the ever-transformational oversoul. If we must usually sense the world by way of the confusing variety of its timebound evanescent material, poetry, from the beginning, has helped us realize what Richard Wilbur has called the "poverty" of thinking things only what they seem to be.

For some years now I've been trying to listen to myself think. One thing I've clearly observed is that my mind leaps to an intuition, a wordless intuition with a sense of knowledge behind it, and then, and only then, do words form to explain and order this intuition. There is the soundless and electrical birth, and then the watery blood-flecked afterbirth of words which usually do not quite seem to surround/embody the intuition, and which are too poor to take as their form the timelessness that engendered them in the first place. Meanwhile, what is it in me observing this process? What is it that sees me when I see myself in a dream? Poetry is that interfusion where "Being passes into Appearance." I would like to read poetry by way of that engendering spiritual entity that both creates and witnesses this miracle.

Emerson tells us that unity has to do with "moral sentiment" constantly sinking into our souls, as though we learn, or should, love and forbearance from all things and all relations at all hours of the day. In *Nature*, his first book, his "wedge," he tells us that nothing is free from partaking of the whole, not "a leaf, a drop, a crystal," and then, in this beautiful series, in its last knock-out phrase, "a moment of time." To understand microcosmically a leaf with its veins and seasons, or a crystal which is the building block of creation, is one thing; but to imagine, to conceive of "a moment of time" as a microcosm is another dimension of realization demanded of us. Imagine: if the moments right now while I am writing this sentence and while you are reading it are indeed indicative of all moments ever, then we are with Jesus on the road to Jerusalem, with Thoreau at Walden Pond, with the victims at Auschwitz and with their murderers—nothing is excluded, we are whole and *liable*, responsible for all the selves we are in time. Any moment in time, Emerson argues, "faithfully renders the likeness of the world." And why do we feel like nodding assent to this provocative assertion? He rushes at us, sentence by sentence, question by question, image by image in a kind of wild sermonic persuasive associative assault. Such passion cannot be mistaken. We're rapt in him. Our lives are eternal and holy. If we plumb, our pipes and sump-pumps will be our bodies in breathing hieroglyph. If we farm, our land will be a mute gospel and we must ready ourselves to awaken and to hear its divine and obvious torah, bible, koran, medicine bundle all uttered at once in a sheep's eyes and in a chicken's feathers, in a beetle's sheen in its pile of moist dung, in the nutritious scent of hay and in the anthrax that might cost us our livelihood.

A Moment Faith

After reading Irving Greenberg's essay "Cloud of Smoke, Pillar of Fire: Judaism, Christianity, and Modernity After the Holocaust," I wrote a poem called "Coin":

> What was a Jewish child worth, summer, 1944,
> when the Nazis halved the dosage of Zyklon B
> from 12 boxes to 6 boxes for each gassing?
>
> When released, the gas rose, forcing the victims
> in their death struggles to fight upward,
> but the gas filled every pocket of air, at last.
>
> What was a Jewish child worth when the Nazis,
> to save money, doubled even this agony
> by halving the gas? 5 marks per kilogram,
>
> 5.5 kilograms invested in every Auschwitz chamberload
> of 1500 units. With the mark at 25 ,
> this meant $6.75 per 1500 units,
>
> or 45/100 of a cent per person. Still,
> this was too much, and sometimes the rationed gas
> ran out during the long queue of consumers,
>
> so children were thrown alive into the furnaces:
> in the summer of 1944 at Auschwitz, a Jewish child
> was not worth a half cent to the Reich
>
> which struck this coin, floating freely upward now
> into that economy, this 25 mark piece,
> one risked mark for each line, gas

for more than 60 children for each line,
if it please God and/or the Nazis in their mercy
at least to gas them before they are heaved

into the flames of the Thousand Year Reich.

Considering the unimaginable crimes of the Nazis against the innocent, Greenberg asks how, after Auschwitz, we can ever speak other than nihilistically, ever live other than faithlessly. Has not the concerned and merciful and just God of History proved himself dead at best, demonic at worst? Is not our world now unredeemable *forever, forever* a place of pain and meaningless defeat?

I think of poetry when Greenberg says, "Let us offer then, as working principle, the following: No statement, theological or otherwise, should be made that would not be credible in the presence of the burning children." ("Credible" in their presence, he says—acceptable to them might be another, more demanding way to put it. Perhaps we must also insist that it must be of interest to them, must not bore them.) Why should we not demand this austere accountability of our poetry?

"After Auschwitz," Greenberg says, "faith means there are times when faith is overcome. . . . We now have to speak of 'moment faiths,' moments when Redeemer and vision of redemption are present, interspersed with times when the flames and the smoke of the burning children blot out faith—though it flickers again." Fully aware of what happened to those people gassed and cremated by the thousands, by the tens and hundreds of thousands, we may ask why we should not curse God and live only to deny Him—only this understandable revulsion and hate would seem to make sense after the horror. But Greenberg says, "The victims ask that we do not jump to a conclusion that retrospectively makes the covenant they lived an illusion and their death a gigantic travesty. . . . The victims ask us, above all, not to allow the creation of another matrix of values that might sustain another attempt at genocide."

Our poems will be "moment faiths" and they will be moment unfaiths. Sometimes we will not know exactly what they are, and we will need to rely on our intuitions and senses of musical resolution and irresolution in order to judge them by Greenberg's proposition, itself, by its own definition, necesssarily open to question. We will need to know our deepest selves in order that we do not lie to ourselves and perpetrate further crimes against the burning children. Please understand, we will say to them when we write something risky, indefinite, suggestive, perhaps surreal, perhaps raving and wild or wrapped in barbed wire, something perhaps on the razor's edge of insanity or obscenity—as the camps were riddled with insanity and obscenity—as we try to honor the victims' eternally inescapable fates. Please understand, we will say to them. But we must be hard on ourselves. But we must not censor ourselves. But we must believe the murdered children are listening. This is the Holocaust's charge to us.

KO

Sometimes I have a general sense of where I'm going—a sound to keep following, or a shape on the page to keep filling out, or a story to work in and round toward, or a shifting combination of these. Sometimes I pretty much end up with what I decided I could or ought to do. But I'm most interested in poems that somehow find themselves somewhere they didn't know they'd be. They remind me of something that boxer Mike Tyson once said: "Everybody's got a plan until they're hit."

I've got a plan, but I'm hit. I'm staggering. I grope for the ropes, I'm hit again. The ropes don't support me, I fall. Maybe I get up and try to get the feeling in my legs back again. Maybe I stay down and out and at the end can't even hear the sound of the bell.

Subject Matter

You're riding a horse, but pretty much giving it its rein. You are borne along by it, can shift your posture in the saddle, can look around you to remark on the landscape, bushes & trees galloping by—are those honeysuckles or redtwig dogwoods, maples or box elders?— but from long habit & imagined necessity you stay on the horse with your feet in the stirrups. You are riding along on your steed named "Subject" when, *wham*, an overhanging branch takes you out. You see stars & wonder, later, what galaxy it was that you visited, and what in hell happened to your horse.

The Crossing

Some years ago, a packed school bus returning late at night from a basketball game collided with a train. Several deaths, many injuries.

At the crossing, there was supposed to be a switchman swinging a lighted lantern to stop any traffic and allow the train through.

In court, the switchman swore he was where he was supposed to be, at the crossing, swinging his lantern long before the train arrived, but swore that the bus driver had ignored him.

The driver of the bus said he saw someone who may have been the switchman at the crossing, but this person did not have a lantern.

The judge first assumed that either the driver or the switchman was lying; then, by way of years of experience and by intuition, he realized that both men might be telling the truth: perhaps the switchman had been there and had been swinging his lantern, but, for whatever reason, the lantern had not been lit.

When is a lantern a lantern? What happens at the crossing? When is a poem a poem?

The Snow Principle

Out of the winter branches, a small brown body, a sparrow's, fluttered toward me, downward in feathery disarray, turning ungracefully in a tumult of legs and wings, and fell at my feet. I saw that it was headless. I guessed that its head had been struck off by an owl or hawk that had seen me and had not followed its meal to the snow. . . .

But this never happened. It looks as though I was the one who struck off the sparrow's head—maybe just to be able to explain one sentence by way of another. And for the pleasure of picture and movement, everything taking place, as always, even in summer, against such snow as this.

Old Topaz

*Form always stands in dread of power. What the devil will he
do next?*

—Emerson

Once there was a fish who couldn't swim. From the time he was
born, he just lay in the gravel in or near—sometimes he managed to
wriggle a little ways away—his parents' nest.

No one could teach Sunny to swim, not the old graywhiskered
catfish who told him to have some pride for once in his life, not the
pickerel with two hooks in his mouth who told him to get his backbone
and tail muscles into the act, not the perch fingerling who told him to
close his eyes and dream he was flying through the blue and white sky
over the pond. No, no one could help him. Sunny just wriggled a little,
scratching his belly on gravel, or lay listless and depressed all day or all
night long, lily pads unfurling, sprites and spiders wrinkling the surface
so unattainably high above him.

His dutiful parents, without complaint, continued to feed him,
expelling bits of tadpole or mayfly or waterbug or tubeworm in front of
him where he could reach them, but he could see in his mother's eyes
that she was heartbroken, in his father's that he was angry.

I noticed all this from a distance. I didn't want to take advantage.
I was more interested, for the time being, in studying someone like
Sunny. I myself lost a foot to a crane when I was young. I was just
minding my business, chewing on duckweed near shore, when a crane
plucked me from the water and severed my foot. I'm lucky to be alive.
I'll never forget what happened to me. Yes, I've known both physical
agony and the mental anguish that is its twin.

Call me Old Topaz, for my eyes. I'm at the top of the food chain
here. Where I tread, I force the pond to rearrange itself around me.

A week ago, a heron waded too close to Sunny. I was hidden there.
I snapped my jaws and broke one of its legs. It shrieked away in dactyllic
painsong. Now it knows what Sunny and I know.

Yesterday noon when lilypad shadows shone straight down and the dark light pleased my eyes, I decided to try scare tactics. I rounded a submerged willow trunk, raised up on my three legs, and stomped directly toward Sunny. When he saw me, my black triangular head, my jewel eyes, he blanched white and flapped backwards pitiably an inch or two. I retreated, knowing I'd failed, but I tried to relieve my gloom: I told myself that maybe Sunny would fall into an exhausted sleep, that chemicals released in him because of his intense fright would heal him, and he'd be swimming by morning. I knew I was lying to myself. But you can't be too hard on yourself, and I gave myself credit for two things: for trying to scare Sunny into swimming, and for lying to myself.

I know that you're thinking that Old Topaz is a strange one, congratulating himself for deluding himself. But the truth is I have a bleeding stomach ulcer—I think it's those damned watersnakes—and if I didn't lie to myself after my Sunny-strategy went bad, I wouldn't have been able to sleep. I slept at least passably. I even had a brief dream: Sunny swam over, kissed my stump in gratitude, and my foot grew back. Ever since a hundred years ago when my mother—may she rest in peace—told me the fable of the lion and the mouse who removed the thorn from the lion king's paw, I've had these dreams in which I'm a do-gooder, or in which, after the fact, someone like Sunny is thanking me for the help I've rendered. My foot has grown back more times than we have dragonflies around here.

This morning, Sunny was the same. He lay unmoving at the center of his parents' nest.

I see that I've already placed Sunny, that little cripple, in the past tense. I know myself better than you might think I do. And I know that life is made up of two elements, power and form, and the proportions must invariably be kept if we want our lives to be sweet and sound. There's no question but that if Sunny doesn't learn to swim soon, I'm going to snap him up just to get him off my mind. For all you know for sure, maybe I already have. Be careful. It wouldn't be the first time.

Three: The Host

The Eggs

I know a place in the Thousand Islands where a turtle came up out of the river to lay her eggs. Oblivious to the vacationers who gathered to watch, she made her way up onto a grassy slope along a marsh near a marina and began digging. She cut through grass with her flippers, got down to soft sand and mud, and dropped her eggs, one by one rolling them under first her right flipper and then her left. Each time she pressed out one of her small, rubbery eggs, her eyes would seem to roll completely around in her head. . . . Hours later, she dragged herself wearily back to water.

Someone put four stakes around that nest to mark it and protect it from the mower. This was maybe six weeks ago. Is there enough heat left this season for the eggs to hatch? Will the baby turtles be able to cut their way up through the compacted soil to the light, and will they be able to reach the water before gulls or coons take them? The nest may already be thickly overgrown with new grass and dandelions that will make it impossible for the hatchlings to surface. I can't check. I was just a tourist. Was the mother following million-year-old instincts to a laying-place that just now in her generation has become untenable? The eggs are there underground within their history of tides and sea life from before the first of our human ancestors. Maybe, even now, the baby turtles' eyes have rotted away; maybe, even now, those eyes are forming and will find their ways into the channel, and then the sea, again.

The New Poem

A news story tells of a hog that tried to have sex with a Harley. Hog to hog. It did a grand's worth of damage. We didn't hear the details, but I picture a compromised gas tank & a lubricated leather seat.

The local authorities have decided that the flesh & blood hog needs to be castrated, but even the Harley's owner has asked for mercy. He says that the pig surely didn't know that having sex with a motor-cycle was against the law.

In James Dickey's poem "The Sheep Child" a farm boy "wild to couple with anything" fathers the forlorn title creature which we might now be able to view in its jar of formaldehyde in a museum, but I like to think of the robust living offspring of the hog & Harley: a rubber snout with which to snort & sing; gristle heart beating in a chest of spokes; breath of gasoline, roses, & turnips; three headlight eyes set far back in its bristled chassis; the intelligence of a machine fused with the appetites of a sow in rut, a boar in heat.

Somewhere in Ohio

I once had a dream that a book and I made love. I won't describe the exact position of this intercourse. The book's leaves lay open, but other details of our difficult and exacting anatomical configurations should be left to your own imagination.

Sounds like a good reason, doesn't it, never to lend anyone one of your treasured books? Who would want to risk such infidelity or violation?

I'm a book collector. Book collectors and their obsessions are an old story, of course. I remember from Holbrook Jackson's famous *Anatomy of Bibliomania* certain collectors who slept on or under their books. But I don't recall anything quite like my dream.

I said that a book and I "made love." I didn't say I simply had sex with this book. When I awoke, I remembered that the experience had not simply been a lusty one. Nor was it in any way violent, or sordid. It was tinged with eroticism, and I woke with feelings of warmth and fulfillment and gratitude because of my relationship with that book.

It's likely, given the shared love of this dream, I knew the book's title, but I lost this knowledge, if I had it, when I opened my eyes. If I now knew the book's title, if it had one, I could better understand what would engender such a dream in me.

What if it was a book by a poet I care for? I happen to be heterosexual—what if this poet were male?

What if this book was a biography of, say, Adolf Hitler? Charlotte Beradt in her *The Third Reich of Dreams* (1968) reports that during and after WWII (and no doubt this phenomenon exists to the present) many survivors had sexual dreams of Hitler rouged, Hitler in a gown, etc. The implications would be voluminous.

What if this book was a biography of, say, Elvis Presley? or Joan of Arc? or my childhood hero Mickey Mantle? What if it was the Bible? or one of my lost books, maybe the copy of Kraft-Ebing's *Psycopathia Sexualis* that I underlined and wrote poems in more than twenty years ago but left behind somewhere in Ohio when I finished graduate school? We usually dream the dream we need for physical and mental health, for balance. Maybe my dream was one of unity and deep understanding, a coming to grips with guilt that had been building in me over the long years of my bookish life.

What if it was a book I myself had written? Or one of the anthologies that I've edited?

Or a book I plan to write? The poet John Logan used to say that when he wrote or read his poems he thought of using his tongue to make love to an audience. Was my dream a hieroglyph of what I felt my relationship with my writing, and maybe my audience, had to come to be?

What if it was a cookbook?

What if it was a book about our western deserts, or about the Amazon and its rainforests? Was my dream a dream of the penetration of nature? Did I want to impregnate Mother Nature herself?

What if it was a book by my friend Raymond Carver who had died a short time before my dream? The possibilities here are so myriad—separations, conjoinings, gratitudes, jealousies, declarations— that they overwhelm my daylight mind.

What if the book was a blank book, the kind in which I keep my journal? I enjoy this probability best of all, my dream becoming a metaphor or parable of the creative process, or maybe an indication of the wished-for perfection of the life over the work.

The English poet and novelist Martin Booth happened recently to send me a book called *Celebrity Book of Dreams*. There's an alphabetical listing of dream images and motifs. This is the entry for "Books":

> (whether in a library or a bookshop) Since books contain ideas, they can be an allegory for the thoughts and memories of the dreamer.

An awfully skimpy entry. Whether in a library or a bookshop. But what about in a bed? In any case, if I knew the book, I would better know my own thoughts and ideas. Since I don't, I wonder if the dream just diffused itself away inconsequentially, or if I've censored myself, afraid to know what is inside the dream-mirror.

In my conscious life, I know myself, my passion, so think that the book must have been, whatever its identity, a first edition, probably in a pristine dust jacket. This is no doubt why I did not—I think I did not—

reach orgasm in this dream. For book collectors, moisture is anathema, of course.

I trust that the book's paper was soft, enfolding. I trust, since many dreams relieve us of death anxiety, that the paper was acid-free.

Maybe, simply, this book was one I'd been looking for for a long time. At last, I'd found it, and was now sharing one of the deepest, most personal, most resonant parts of my life with it. We can't always find all the books we want, and can't always own them when we find them. For once, maybe, my yearning had reached the point at which I needed a dream of active but loving union.

And what could the offspring of such an immaculate union of dreamer and book be? What else? A new life. A story, or a poem, or such an indulgence as this.

Inspiration: The Locker

Leona leaned against her locker, feeling faint. Maybe it was all those chemicals in chemistry lab, those muddy green smells. Maybe it was a flu coming on. She wondered if she should report to the nurse's office. But she was a very conscientious student, and wanted, if possible, to finish the day.

The hall was emptying for the beginning of fifth period. Mr. Krassner, her English teacher, stood outside his classroom door and saw her.

"Leona?"

"Yes."

"You okay?"

"Yes." Leona walked toward him. When she reached him, she swooned and slid to the floor like a suddenly wilted sunflower.

That's the way Mr. Krassner would put it to his last two classes of the day: "Little blonde Leona swooned at my feet like a suddenly wilted sunflower."

But Leona was fine by the next day—it must have been food poisoning or some kind of 24-hour bug. Or those smells from chemistry lab or the smells of the disinfectant wash that Mr. Jacobi, custodian, had used in the halls the night before Leona had gotten sick. In any case, we're almost done with her. She appears punctually every day for Mr. Krassner's class. She goes on with her life in the active tense, and life happens to her in the passive. For all we know, she lives another eighty years. That would be another eighty stories, or eight thousand, at least.

We're almost done with Mr. Krassner, too. Between classes, he keeps checking the hall, then steps inside his classroom and goes on with his lessons. Maybe WWII comes along and he enlists or, since his isn't a critical occupation, he's drafted. "Medic, medic!" a soldier screams from the black volcanic sands of Iwo Jima, and Krassner crawls on his elbows and belly toward his duty. Maybe.

But we're not done with Elliott. He's the one who had once planted several rows of sunflowers and had watched them grow until they were taller than he was. He's the one who experienced what Mr. Krassner said: "Little blonde Leona swooned at my feet like a suddenly wilted sunflower." Elliott's whole brain lit up when he heard this, lit up like his tongue when he drank lemon pop.

Elliot kept a looseleaf diary. In his diary that weekend he began to fall in love with Leona. But it was not her. We are done with her, and so is Elliott, though Elliott does not yet know this. His diary begins to bloom with sunflower words—not these: *corolla, whip-slender stem, seed-whorl, crook-neck, petal-curl, head-weight, sepal-burst;* not these, but words just the same, and his. In one way or another, his sunflower words are not about Leona, though he thinks they are.

It's a long weekend for him. Too bad it's winter and the ground is frozen. The ground is so smooth and hard it can remind you of the hall floors that Mr. Jacobi just keeps washing with that smelly stuff and polishing with that milky stuff.

It's a long weekend for Elliott, but Monday arrives at last. He has his diary with him in English class. He detaches some of his recent entries—where does he find the courage?—and slips them onto Leona's desk.

Actually, she doesn't know what to make of them. They make her feel a little dizzy. "Elliott?" she says.

Her embarrassment and confusion humiliate him, though she does not mean to. That evening, he writes a dozen more pages in his diary, pages no one will ever see, and then over the next fifty years composes and publishes five or fifteen books of poetry, the first of which is dedicated to Mr. Krassner. . . .

Mr. Jacobi leans on his mop in the hall outside what was once Mr. Krassner's classroom. He enjoys the clean, antiseptic smell of the floorwash as he has for so many years, and appreciates, tonight, the way moonlight streaks the tiles. He's always been of a contemplative turn of mind. If only these lockers could talk, he thinks, I bet they'd have some stories to tell.

Moonlight glances up from the tiles through louvers into the black air of one locker, this one.

Mr. Jacobi begins mopping again, right, left, right, left, the arc-shapes he likes. When he reaches a certain point in the hall, his pail blocks moonlight and the air in what was once Elliott's locker goes black.

Ecology

Stencilled in red paint in block letters on many lockers where I change to play basketball three times a week is the legend PRIVATE LOCKS ARE NOT ALLOWED ON LOCKERS. I've seen these thirty-four letters for years, and with some part of my mind I've read their injunction each time I've suited up. Since I've been law-abiding and have gotten my own duly-registered lock legally from the recreation desk, I've not had to pay close attention.

But today I was early for ball, sat on a bench to kill time, and focussed on the seven words. In my mind I shortened them to NO PRIVATE LOCKS ALLOWED ON LOCKERS, then to NO PRIVATE LOCKS ON LOCKERS, then simply to NO PRIVATE LOCKS (there being nothing else to lock in this locker room but lockers). I thought of going to an image of a lock with a line drawn through it, but this might be confusing, there being no easily-recognizable generic symbol for a private lock. NO PRIVATE LOCKS is about as direct a message as possible, four words/twenty letters shorter than the muzzy sentence currently emblazoned every six feet around the room. NO PRIVATE LOCKS as operative phrase does have its problems: in philosophical and deconstructive academia it might suggest that private locks do not exist; the PRIVATE could be read as a noun, the LOCKS as a verb, and the three words together seem to ROTC students another in a series of endless enigmatic directives from a command that labels pencils Communications Media #1. In short, I realized that my three chosen words were subject to fuzzy and foolish interpretation, as are all human utterances. But NO PRIVATE LOCKS is hewn about as close to the spirit of the desired communication as I can hope to get, and, if misunderstood, would have to be almost *wilfully* misunderstood.

When the lockers are repainted, the seven words should in every case be replaced with my three, and I shall write to the president of my college, the Chancellor of the State University of New York, and to individual members of the Board of Trustees to suggest this change. The three words, for one thing, are more emphatic and direct, are likely to get better results than the wimpy ungainly passive of the seven-word original. Also, unnecessary and meaningless labor will be eliminated, freeing the stenciller for more important tasks, then freeing the maintenance staff from having to saw off private locks, thus lessening the pressure on a work force that especially during these times of fiscal crisis must be employed efficiently. In turn, the manufacturer will be freed from having to produce more locks to replace those that were cut off— the manufacture of locks and of everything else made of metal increases the severity of the carcinogenic siege on our bodies. In the same way, my revision will reduce the use of toxic paint, and the college at one and the same time will fulfill its ethical obligation to budget only for supplies that are absolutely necessary. My change will also reduce mental and visual pollution. Health care costs would in the long run be reduced.

The Governor might want to award me a Citizen's Medal, but I would refuse, the manufacture of such a medal necessarily resulting in the same pollution as the manufacture of locks.

Imagine having to hear or read just three words for every seven on this campus: my day clarifies; I say in class the thing itself that I have been wanting to say for decades; my poem realizes its ability to save a forest. Committee meetings become tolerable. And in my locker room daydream I am able to linger a while longer, long enough to see that the people who manufactured the toxic paint have left the city and gone back to farming for good.

Notes Toward a Grub Poetics

This morning, a tribe of feathered hunters prickles my lawn, spearing grubs.

The starlings must be union workers. In their contract: *Do not sing. Eat grubs.*

The grubs are white, juicy & soft. Plucked from minuscule holes, they seem to expand into whole beakfuls.

Links in The Great Chain of Being, starlings shit in the grass. Soon, by its root-hairs, grass absorbs the nutritious starling shit. In spring, as today, grubs rise to eat grassroots. They fatten. They fill the bellies of starlings that shit in the grass.

Each starling can see through two eyes, except for the one whose one socket is as white as a grub.

Not one grub is a bishop, mullah, or rabbi, so far as we know. Not one is an athlete, so far as we know. Not one is a rock star. Not one is electable, not one commutes from the suburbs to Wall Street, not one arms itself or thinks with its blood-gorged dick, so far as we know.

The starlings do not realize they are a non-indigenous species. In their dreams, do they see their Asian homeland? Coming or going, they are always at home.

What I do not know about starlings & grubs reminds me of the way they do not walk but seem to lurch & stumble from grub to grub.

Starlings are neither infidels nor believers among the dandelion heads under the sycamore under the gold wheel of the great sun.

If there are more lawns with grubs in them than there are grubs in any one lawn, & there are; if there are more trees than there are leaves on any one tree, & there are: then there must be many trees with exactly the same number of leaves; then there must be lawns with exactly the same number of grubs.

Grubs that survive will become winged buzzing creatures in the trees.

Pig Notes

Empiricism

At the Orleans County Fair I was looking into a pigsty when its proprietor threw in a pailful of soggy vegetables and spoiled fruit. The sty's several inhabitants snorted and pushed and rolled in muck, competing for this fare. I heard a child who was looking on say, "Yeeks, what pigs, no wonder they call them pigs."

Utilitarianism

In another sty, a pig was snouting around a perfect pigtoy. What toy couldn't be chewed or eaten or knocked out of the pen? What was safe and indestructible and heavy enough to provide the pig exercise? What would roll when pushed as though alive? The pig was snouting around a bowling ball.

O Sages of Concord

At Brook Farm in 1841—I see him as though in a movie—Nathaniel Hawthorne is staring down into a pen, meditating on several of the community's swine: "I suppose it is the knowledge that these four companions are doomed to die within two or three weeks that gives them a sort of awfulness in my conception. It makes me contrast their sudden gross substance of fleshly life with the nothingness speedily to come. . . . They appear the more a mystery the longer one gazes at them. It seems as if there were an important meaning to them, if one could but find it out. . . ."

Nathaniel is baffled and intrigued by the evanescence of pighood—he senses some kind of swine transcendentalism—but you and I, too far from the ideals of Brook Farm, are not particularly interested in these grunters. We know that pigs mean what they are, that what they are and what they provide—their own utilitarianism—are the same, whether or not we can say it. Lights, camera, action: knuckles, chops, bacon.

The Muse

In another sty, a boar was rooting in slop beneath its mate's body. Having had her fill earlier, she was sleeping, but the boar kept snouting beneath her body, at one point almost rolling her over. He didn't care about her own plans for the afternoon. And that snuffling noise made us think he felt close to discovering a field of truffles. But she kept at her sleeping, and he never managed, this time, to turn her over or even get her attention.

The Muse

1.

In my dream an old woman in a European mountain village is brought to where a body has been found in the ice of melting spring.

She is brought to this place through grasses, snow-patches, first wild-flowers. The villagers stand in a circle around her as she views the body. Yes, it is her betrothed who fell into a chasm sixty years before. . . .

2.

His young face is wet & shining, he has not aged a day since his accident. The woman kneels beside him, rosaries twined in her fingers, her face a guttering candle as she prays.

3.

You and I, witnesses, wonder what, if anything, will happen next.

The Feather

This story takes place in a village set in a forest.

A man is sitting in the corner of a *Gasthaus*. He looks out over a ravine to the pines beyond. When he was a boy, he remembers, he once saw a nest of eagles in those pines. Now, only crows sometimes alight in the highest branches, watching the village, maybe creating it in their eyes as they see it, sometimes crying out, *rawr, rawr*.

Today, he is alone. Even the barkeep must be sleeping in the back room. Even the cook must be slumped in a corner of the kitchen. The waitress has not yet arrived, or has already gone home. The light is uncertain this time of day, whatever time it is. And today there are no crows in the heights of the distant pines, and no sounds. He stares toward the forest, lost not in any thought that employs words, but in wordless reverie, as close to sleep as we are when we spiral to this forest, this village, this *Gasthaus*, this man who seems to be waiting for something to happen.

Did he see her? A woman, was it? Dressed in green as though she were a small tree that had uprooted itself from the forest. She walked toward him, toward the ravine, and descended, her hat disappearing from view.

It must have been his imagination, he thinks. My *imagination*, are the exact words he says to himself as he blinks himself awake. But a woman was there, wasn't she? He can still picture her hat with its single feather disappearing as she descended the ravine. . . .

How long should he wait for her to reappear? Should he change his life? He could leave the *Gasthaus* and stand at the edge of the ravine to look for her. He could climb down into the ravine itself. My *imagination*, he assures himself.

The Host

I think of a friend's study of a New Guinea weevil in the field. He tells me that when the insect matures it rolls over to gather a pod of soil on its moist back. The soil eventually sprouts algaes, lichens, mosses, microscopic ferns, mushrooms. Mites & pinhead snails & tiny maurauding slugs take up residence in this miniature jungle, this whole ecosystem that the weevil bears on its back for camouflage &, no doubt, for other benefits still mysteries to us. The host seems even to regulate the weather of this world, touching it to dew, sunning it, shading it. Like a work of the imagination, when the weevil dies, the world on its back absorbs it, recycles itself, keeps saying itself down through time.

Ambiguity

Reaching the last stanza of the anonymous old ballad "Barbara Allan"—

> "O mother, mother, make my bed!
>   O make it saft and narrow!
> Since my love died for me today,
>   I'll die for him tomorrow."—

I was swept back for understanding to the tavern scene of the fifth stanza (in the version I was reading) in which Barbara explains why she has no pity for John, who is dying a love-death for her:

> "O dinna ye mind, young man," said she,
>   "When ye was in the tavern a-drinking,
> That ye made the healths gae round and round,
>   And slighted Barbara Allan?"

Here, in the fifth of nine stanzas, the center of the poem, we hear of the incident that generates the whole poem, forwards (towards John's death and Barbara's subsequent death) and backwards (John is deathly sick to begin with because Barbara spurns him, and she spurns him because of what she perceives to be this tavern slight or insult).

But my recognition—first intuitive and then put into words—while finishing the poem was that while I could trace the lives of these two characters to *something* that happened in the tavern, I still could not know what it was, or what fifty things it was, that led to such a tragic outcome (the poem is based on real deaths, I take it, and is not just hyperbolic story-telling). Walter Jackson Bate and David Perkins in their note in *British & American Poets: Chaucer to the Present* mention the "starkness or absence of detail that activates imagination and creates poignance" in such ballads. Another way to think of this is in poet Tess Gallagher's terms: "A diminishment of reality takes place when our experience is negotiated without ambiguity. . . . This ambiguity [in poetry] permits the spectator to insert details of his or her own, niches of perception left undertermined or open by the artist." (Hemingway and others, of course, have spoken of the writer's need to have a feeling for what to leave out.) My recognition was that were I Sir John in that tavern, were I smitten by Barbara, I might not have made her health go round and round because I was too shy, or because I wanted to play it cool, or because I was dizzy in love and forgetful of outer circumstances but drank to Barbara wordlessly with every swallow, or because I was drunk, or because she was not of my social level and it wouldn't have been good for either of us to draw attention to the fact that I loved her, or for reasons so complex (my need for suffering, e.g.) that I myself couldn't begin to fathom them. Interstices here for me, all buzzing in me simultaneously with that instant of poetry, that moment of full awareness created in me by all the elements of the ballad coming together. "Don't you remember?" ("dinna ye mind") asks Barbara—oh, how long did she cherish, for complex reasons of her own, this sweet poisonous memory before injecting John with it?

Sir John cannot/will not answer Barbara's charge. At the beginning of the sixth stanza, "He turned his face unto the wall, / And death was with him dealing." All he can say is "Adieu" to his friends and ask them to be kind to Barbara. The balladeer leaves John speechless after Barbara's revelation. "And slowly, slowly raise she up, / And slowly left him." As, reluctantly, I leave this poem, its rhythms cling to me, become part of my heartbeat, "slowly, slowly." There is too much, or nothing, to explain.

Roseville

Karen Dunkle had been browsing Paradise Mall's annual antique show and sale. She'd been looking carefully at a piece of Roseville pottery she was thinking of buying—a small blue bowl in the white rose pattern from the '40s, an object you could turn in your hands to feel the cyclic pattern of roses and vines in their imperishable frieze—but was that a chip in its base or just a natural kiln-fleck of some kind that wouldn't affect its value?—she'd been browsing and concentrating on white roses when Konrad Glimmerman, walking past her, slipped on a spot of mustard and knocked her forward against three tiers of glassware and pottery while he himself fell not on his back with his feet thrown up in front of him as is usually depicted in slapstick cartoons, but, somehow, as we've observed, to Karen's side, his left leg striking her in the back of her knees so that she seemed, as the antique glassware and pottery swept over them in a wave of shards and slivers, to be planning to sit on Konrad, which she did. By the time the smashing and tinkling of breakage had stopped, when the last carnival glass tumbler had rolled to a still-point and the last cut-glass ashtray had stopped cracking and spinning, Karen—the Roseville bowl that Konrad would later buy for her intact in her hands—looked down at Konrad, who was afraid to move, and said, "I don't believe we've been introduced."

To make a long story short, it is a week later. By now, Karen and Konrad have exhausted all jokes about their first meeting, have told and retold those few seconds to both circles of their friends in such slow motion and with so many variations that it seemed only natural to them that Karen should end up sitting on Konrad's buttocks in Paradise Mall in the way she had, bits of amethyst glass sequinned on her bouffant— miraculously, however uncomfortable such fleeting notoriety might have made them, neither had been even slightly hurt during this adventure—while Konrad could think only of the dog ordure into which he must, he thought, have stepped, could only hope that said dreck was not beneath him at that very moment. After three dates, Karen and Konrad have worn the story out. In fact, they swear to one another that they will never again tell this story to themselves or anyone else, that it will remain their own silent secret, that if they ever argue or find themselves glum or heartbroken they will look at one another and smirk, knowing what the other is remembering.

To make a very long story much shorter, however, we now see them on their golden anniversary. As life would have it, it is after dinner and frail Karen is standing at a microphone behind a three-tiered wedding cake at the Senior Center, which their children and friends have rented for the celebration. Just tall enough to see over the cake, she is looking out at this congregation and beginning to say a few words. Konrad, who broke his left hip a few months before, forgetful now and beginning to lose track of things, prone to wandering aimlessly about, stands up from his chair at the head table and begins walking behind Karen. A curve of blue begins to form in the back of his mind. He is thinking of telling a story.

The Apple

Eat with me, as apparently we are meant to, the fruit of William Blake's "A Poison Tree":

> I was angry with my friend:
> I told my wrath, my wrath did end.
> I was angry with my foe:
> I told it not, my wrath did grow.
>
> And I water'd it in fears,
> Night and morning with my tears;
> And I sunned it with smiles,
> And with soft deceitful wiles.
>
> And it grew both day and night,
> Till it bore an apple bright;
> And my foe beheld it shine,
> And he knew that it was mine,
>
> And into my garden stole
> When the night had veil'd the pole:
> In the morning glad I see
> My foe outstretch'd beneath the tree.

The fruit of the speaker's wrath, the "apple bright," has swelled into ripeness twenty-four hours a day, succulent with the speaker's fears, tears, smiles and wiles. The poem, itself a poison tree, grows this fruit. It hangs heavily in the lower boughs of the tree and in our mind's eye as we lure our foe to the red (somehow *so* red) apple. By morning, our enemy is dead, dead at last. We are glad. Our fears, tears, smiles, wiles are now part of *his* poisoned body, he has partaken of us. The poem ends in joy.

And there is nothing within it to undercut this joy. It does not seem to tell us to be open with our foe, from the beginning, so that the poison tree cannot root in us. It does not tell us to forgive. Unless we impose a contrary moral code on the poem, the poison tree lights up the morning. The death of our foe—and a foe is here as natural as a friend—seems to redeem all our time and suffering.

But of course this is itself Blake's strategy. He assumes our common humanity, and we become accomplices in this murder. When we participate, when we find joy, we ourselves have taken and eaten the bright green (somehow *so* green) fruit of a poison tree. We are ourselves our foe, and will die. We went through so much—such perverted nurturing—to grow this tree, but are ourselves in the end our own victims. This is a suicide poem, a suicide note we have composed about ourselves.

To notice context, too: "The Human Abstract," an earlier poem in *Songs of Experience,* is more directly dark and less intriguing than "A Poison Tree." Here our tree "bears the fruit of Deceit, / Ruddy and sweet to eat: / And the Raven his nest has made/ In its thickest shade." This tree, Blake says, grows "in the Human Brain." In this way, hedging his bets, he readies us for the deceitful fruit of our brains as we climb down into the better, more dangerous, more faithful poem.

She

Hereabouts, about a hundred years ago, a farmer, a recent widower who had lost interest in money, was being sought by police who wanted to serve warrants on him. Not wanting to be judged or jailed, he started out to seclude himself from the rest of the world. With pick & shovel he began to dig under the protruding root of a huge elm, down several feet into the ground & then toward his woods which were about a hundred yards from his barn. Day after day he continued digging, & day after day the police continued in their attempts to find him.

Finally, after weeks of hard labor, the small hole under the elm developed into a tunnel a hundred yards long. The farmer so concealed its entrance that only he knew where to lift that root. At the end of the tunnel he constructed an up-to-date underground living quarters where he stored provisions to last as long as might ever be necessary. The police kept coming with their warrants, but each visit went for naught. They would even work in shifts & park on the farmer's doorstep for days at a time, but the farmer would withdraw to the far end of his tunnel & remain there until the law scrammed.

More than once, too, the police scoured his woods. He'd hear them above him, raise the wick on his lamp for spite, & laugh, then go back to the diary he was said to have kept. . . .

He was never apprehended. His disappearance became the talk of the countryside. Everyone suspected that he was still on the premises, but where?

The farmer was never found. His tunnel's entrance may have been seen about fifty years ago when a hurricane uprooted the elm, but no other news of that day survives. A rumor persists that the farmer's voluminous diary is packed away in an attic, hereabouts.

Blackberries

Emerson's whole emotional and intellectual life may be seen as his effort to apprehend and live by what he calls the "doctrine of the perpetual revelation." There are innumerable instances in his writings when he challenges accepted truths distant from the experiential present, ones that need to be understood in historical contexts, ones based on superstition or scholarly evidence confused with dumb faith and habit.

Whitman would exclaim, "There was never more inception than there is now, / Nor any more youth or age than there is now," but his Concord master had broken open into this ecstatic idea, one waiting for him in eastern literature and elsewhere, long before, at least as early as the fall of 1826 when he was reading, according to Robert D. Richardson, Jr., in *Emerson: The Mind on Fire* (1995), a little 91-page book by one Samson Reed called *Observation on the Growth of the Mind* (1826). Reed seemed to distill in Emerson thoughts and feelings that to this point had been in foment. Now, in Reed's obliteration of any space between God and the individual soul, in his declaration that "it were fitter to account every moment of the existence of the universe as a new creation, and all as a revelation proceeding each moment from the divinity to the mind of the observer," we realize that we are even now in the unfolding presence of the primal, of essence. All *was* and all *becomes*, but at center all *is*. Creation is an eye creating the present as it sees. Emerson, ten years later in an infamous trope in *Nature*, would describe himself as a transparent eyeball, i.e., not primarily as seer but as *being seen through* by a cosmos of intuition and design—a wild image of present awareness if there ever was one.

Yes, yesterday here in western New York State on acres just a few hundred feet north of the Erie Canal, eastward along which the aged hero of the American Revolution the Marquis de Lafayette sailed in 1823 to kneel and kiss his comrade George Washington's lead coffin—and later, by chance, in Brooklyn, to happen to hold a four-year-old boy by the name of Walter Whitman in his arms—I picked several quarts of blackberries. Today my wife has transformed them into a dozen jars of jam. Months from now, on cold winter mornings, I will spread jam on toast and will taste and smell blackberry summer, remember thorns and leaf-rasp, hear bees and wasps buzzing around me, and those mornings too will become their own present, but right now, the jars of jam cooling, history, future, geography recede. For a few spelled moments as these thoughts form in me, at first wordlessly, I am all revelation, all blackberryness.

Notes on the Moon in Moving Water

> *The history of poetry, oral and written, in all languages, may be rendered in terms of humankind's ongoing conversation with the moon.*
>
> —Edwina Seaver

Notes on the poem of the moon in the river.

Clear night, looking downward into the river, just this once nothing to pester us—no chill or oppressive heat, no gnats or mosquitoes, no pain—the full moon scudding along in the same place in its reflection.

This moon has no dark side.

We cannot walk on it.

We *can* walk on it. It is winter, a foot of ice, water moving beneath us.

We cannot walk on it. It is not in that place on the water where from here it seems to be, fish do not rise into its wavery resonance as they might into a flashlight beam. When we wade out to it in summer, or walk across the ice in winter, it recedes until it reaches the other shore, & then reappears behind us where it has always been.

A passing heron sees it but does not associate it with that huge luminescence high above.

A thrown stone momentarily disperses it, but it soon assumes its trembling form again.

A bag of refuse bobs in the current, passes through the moon, & disappears. . . .

Dip your pen or paintbrush into the moon in the river, & write &/ or paint like crazy, why not, but do not dip your cup into it & drink unless you boil this moonwater first, O sentimentalist.

A moon made of light weighs about as much as a thought in time. It has about the thickness of a new poem held in mind but not yet written down. The moon in our heaven weighs no more than the moon in our river.

A famous writer said that "Women live on the moon, men on the earth," but anyone can live on this moon in this river.

The moon does not break the water. It is not porous, does not get wet, does not erode to gravel & pumice. It does not remember water even as it passes through in its staying, daylight or dark.

The moon is not conscious of itself or its beholder. It is not a brain.

In all the volume of the river's water, there is no particular place where the moon does not shine, even beneath overhanging branches.

> A man saw the moon on the ground in front of him. He picked it up—it was luke-cold—& put it in his briefcase, & went to work with it.
>
> On the subway river, his briefcase on his lap, he wanted to tell others what he had, but they were busy with their newspapers & electronic communications gear.
>
> Arrived at work, he carried his briefcase into his office, placed it under his desk, sometimes leaned his knee into it. When he did, his kneecap tingled, & he knew the moon was still there & hadn't played tricks on him.
>
> All that day & night up to now, he couldn't/can't think of any good reason, coming or going, not to keep that moon to himself, at least for the present.

When a fish splashes in the river, every drop of water contains the moon. Every eye of every fish in the river contains the moon. Every scale.

The moon heats the river, immeasureably.

The moon writes its language on the river with invisible ink. In the future long ago, we once heard a translation.

The moon in the river seems to be practicing zazen, but don't let it fall asleep, hit it with a bamboo stick!

The moon in the river is silent, is a prodigious listener, especially now that your own ear begins to travel with it along its course.

If the river were an image of time & we swam into it, we wouldn't not ever be older, would we? If the moon were an image of enlightenment, it wouldn't not be a lot brighter than it is in our minds right now, would it?

The moon has already found what it is not looking for in the river, but keeps not finding it.

Here, there, everywhere at once, this moon in the river, but us?— only the shadow of the bo tree, a deserted mosque, the ruins of an abbey.

The Buffalo

Had the herds roamed the moon,
we could have seen them
in the clear night sky,

rivers of black light
flowing and emptying
into the sea.

At a carnival, a goldfish in a bowl looks out toward us & blows bubbles, then keeps swimming inside the moon in this water that moves because the goldfish keeps swimming.

Place your pole into the moon in the river & vault it!

The moon is arrow. Bull's eye everywhere!

Does the moon in the river have a home? Does your soul have a home?

Notes on the poem of the moon in the river.

The Garden, The Poem

Spring in Kyoto when a master told a young monk from the city to watch over a flower garden. The monk was grateful for this charge, could feel the garden aspiring upward with his own being in the lilies and unfolding roses and the blossoms of the laden plum tree under which he sat to meditate after he put down each morning's labor, which he felt to be the shaping of beauty. All spring and into summer he watered and pinched, worked among the flowers as though, he thought with pleasure, he were one of the butterflies that blew through the garden like silk handkerchiefs or spiritualized fragments of colored wind.

After mid-summer, during an imperfect meditation, he noticed holes in some leaves of the plum tree above him. He stood up to examine the tree more closely, and saw that caterpillars, ugly hairy things with voracious appetites, were despoiling the tree. Alarmed, he plucked them one by one and crushed them underfoot until the grass beneath the tree was dented with the marks of his foot and colored with the burst bodies of caterpillars.

Seeing that the young monk had unknowingly ruined the garden's beauty, the master took him to another tree where caterpillars were finishing weaving cocoons in the branches. He asked the young monk to sit in meditation under those branches until all seasons were one and he could answer the unasked koan of nature.

Acknowledgments

"On an Archaic Torso of Apollo," "The Wool," Section xvii of "Lord Dragonfly," eight lines from "Brockport, N.Y.: Beginning with 'And,'" "The Host," "A Jar," "Coin," and "The Buffalo" are from *The Host: Selected Poems 1965-1990* (St Louis: Time Being Books, 1994). Copyright © 1994 Time Being Press. Reprinted by permission. Other of William Heyen's poems here first appeared in *The Seneca Review* ("Seneca Country"), *Raccoon* ("Sheep This Evening"), *Skywriting* ("The Eternal Ash"), *TriQuarterly* ("The New American Poetry"), and *Poetry* ("Post-Mortem: Literary Criticism"). "Ensoulment" was first published as a broadside by William B. Ewert (Concord, NH: 1983).

The story "The Village" first appeared in *The Fiction Review*. "Roseville" first appeared in *The Ontario Review* and was reprinted in *Flash Fiction*, edited by James Thomas, Denise Thomas, and Tom Hazuka (New York: Norton, 1992).

The essays "Subject Matter," "Process," "Genius," "The Goose," "The Cop," and "The Bear" were first published in *Desperate Act*. "Rilke: A Little Stone" first appeared in *New Myths/Mss*. "A Moment Truth" (under the title "Coin") first appeared in *Mississippi Valley Review*. "At the Gate" first appeared in *The Chaminade Review*; "Cereal Craft" (under the title "The Banana Parable") in *The Cream City Review*. "Tongues" first appeared in *American Poetry Review*, and is reprinted from *Crazy Horse in Stillness* (Rochester, NY: BOA Editions, Ltd., 1996). "Open Letter to the SUNY Brockport College Community" and "The Host: An Address to the Faculty at SUNY Brockport" also first appeared in *American Poetry Review*. "Notes Toward a Grub Poetics," "Pig Notes," and "The Host" first appeared in *The Ohio Review*; "Seneca Country" in *Witness*. "Old Sam Peabody" was first published as *Our Song*, a broadside presented on Sept. 22, 1988 by the New Hampshire Science Teachers Association to William B. Ewert. "Pickerel" first appeared in *Beneath a Single Moon: Buddhism in Contemporary American Poetry*, edited by Kent Johnson and Craig Paulenich (Boston: Shambhala, 1991).

About the Author

William Heyen was born in Brooklyn, New York, in 1940. He is currently Professor of English and Poet in Residence at the State University of New York at Brockport. A former Senior Fulbright Lecturer in American Literature in Germany, he has won awards and fellowships from the National Endowment for the Arts, the Guggenheim Foundation, *Poetry* magazine, and the American Academy and Institute of Arts and Letters. His work has appeared in *Harper's, The New Yorker, American Poetry Review, TriQuarterly, The Southern Review, The Ohio Review, The Nation, The Ontario Review*, and in many anthologies.

William Heyen is the editor of *American Poets in 1976* and *The Generation of 2000: Contemporary American Poets*. His books of poetry include *Depth of Field, Long Island Light: Poems and a Memoir, Erika: Poems of the Holocaust, Ribbons: The Gulf War, Pterodactyl Rose: Poems of Ecology*, and *The Host: Selected Poems 1965–1990. Crazy Horse in Stillness*, published by BOA Editions, Ltd., was awarded the 1997 National Small Press Book Award for Poetry.

Heyen's cycle of 321 poems, *Diana, Charles, & the Queen* (completed before Princess Diana's death) will appear from BOA in 1998.

Index of Names and Titles

Colophon

Pig Notes & Dumb Music: Prose on Poetry, by William Heyen,
was published in an initial printing of 2,000 copies,
1,950 of which were bound in paper for sale to the trade.
Fifty copies were bound in French papers and quarter cloth,
signed and numbered by the author, of which 40 copies are for sale.

The text was typeset by Richard Foerster, York Beach, Maine,
using Goudy, Amazone, and Futura fonts.
The cover was designed by Daphne Poulin-Stofer,
Rochester, New York.
Manufacturing was by McNaughton & Gunn,
Ann Arbor, Michigan.

BOA EDITIONS, LTD.
AMERICAN READER SERIES